I0690234

Tanner Blue

Acclaim for Valerie Haynes Perry's *Tanner Blue*
Winner of the National Best Books 2008 Award
Fiction & Literature/African American Fiction
Sponsored by USA Book News, October 20, 2008

When I showed the home and neighborhood of Henry O. Tanner to Valerie during our Walking The Spirit Tour in Paris, I never thought that she would run with the inspiration, never mind come up with this beautiful book. *Tanner Blue* is a poetic, honest force to invite into your heart and creative space. Henry O. would have been honored. And now I can include Valerie's novel on the tours.

Julia Browne
CEO and founder, Walking The Spirit Tours

Tanner Blue proved to be a much-needed opportunity to explore a different world.
Paule Marshall
MacArthur Fellow and author of *The Chosen Place, the Timeless People*

Tanner Blue is a mystical, magical book about the creative process. Valerie Haynes Perry has given us a novel rich in allegory and symbolism, but grounded in contemporary daily life. The book moves with the freedom of jazz as Perry brilliantly portrays the paradox of creativity and discipline necessary to any artist in any medium.
Pat Schneider
Author, *Writing Alone & With Others,* Oxford University Press, 2003

Tanner Blue is a very wise and compelling story. I think the book works like a "spirit guide" in its way of showing and suggesting how we can open ourselves to everything we can imagine.
Darryl Vance
Artist and designer

Valerie Haynes Perry has created a novel of deep symbolism with a beautiful character who discovers her inner depths. From the very beginning, I knew I was on a unique journey within a wholly original universe. Images first appear as "ordinary" elements of the story, but before long, the reader knows to pay careful attention to everything.
Maureen Buchanan Jones
Leader of creative writing workshops, poet, and author of *Maud & Adelaide*

Tanner Blue is an extremely powerful, almost hypnotic story. The writing is more akin to poetry than to prose. I was moved by passages of extreme beauty, some of which could stand alone as fine poems.
Ilene Sterns
Artist/photographer

Tanner Blue

a novel

by Valerie Haynes Perry

Copyright © 2008 by Valerie Haynes Perry

All rights reserved. No part of this book may be reproduced or transmitted in any form or by any means, electronic or mechanical, including photocopying, recording, or by any information storage and retrieval system, without the written permission of the author, except where permitted by law.

ISBN: 978-0-6152-3708-4

Cover design and photography by Frederick Douglass Perry
Cover painting by Valerie Haynes Perry
Interior text design by The Word Process

Fiction/African American Literature
Second Edition, 2008

Tanner Blue is available at lulu.com/tannerblue

Dedicated to those who raised me:

Lang C. Haynes, Jr., Eleanor Inniss Haynes, Kenny,

and Aunt Lee

"Refuge maps its own direction."

–Blackton

PART
One

~1~

Low clouds crept over ridges as if sneaking up on time. Peering deeply into the present, the clouds tumbled over hills, swayed above streams and meadows bound for the cliffs of Tourmaline Beach. Finding refuge there, the clouds lingered cautiously above the Pacific ocean, confusing north-coast cliffs with fog. Tiptoeing, they circled the small, one-story house where Tanner Blue drifted between two worlds that whispered her to life.

Get me out of here! I can't breathe anymore!

Great, strong hands held her head and neck, slid along her back, catching her, yet powerless to stop the sinking sensation of falling down to earth. Forceful kicks and strokes made oars of her legs and arms, delivering her from the sooner place into a dusky river of awareness.

Wait — please! I didn't mean that. I don't want to leave....

Tanner Blue clamped both hands to her mouth, vaguely certain that the wailing came from some crowded cavern deep inside her soul. She was unable to stop the rapids tumbling past her eyes, her lips dammed by the bridge her fingers formed across them — unable to stop her roommate, Nile Rive, from blasting into her room on the crest of the determined storm that stirred around them. Studying him, Tanner saw something of herself she could not name. Had it always been there or was it new, like the fetal day exploring formalities of feet?

Leaping from the bed, she wrapped her arms around the buoy of Nile's body, fists clenched tighter than an ancient knot. Her gray, thermal pants and matching, long-sleeved top absorbed the extra warmth of his body. The waves in Tanner's allspice-colored hair, slightly darker than her skin and one shade lighter than Nile's, grazed his broad shoulders. The only time she had touched him before was when they shook hands in agreement that he would rent the extra room on the other side of her house, six months ago.

Adrenaline froze her arms around him as he stood tall in a green flannel shirt and faded jeans. A black braid, fastened with a red elastic band measured his neck. Nile's neat, short beard and well-trimmed moustache defined the smooth angles of his cheeks and chin. It was his even, steady breathing that calmed Tanner. The rhythm of his voice anchored her senses to the present like the ticking of a tireless clock.

Head against Nile's chest, Tanner Blue closed her eyes tightly trying to remember and forget the great, big feeling that stirred her awake, taken with its own importance. The feeling loomed above her like Hokusai's *Wave* ready to pounce, protect, or smother. The need for air forced her eyes open, revealing surroundings rendered unfamiliar. Oxygen filtering through the narrow opening of the green-tinted, sliding glass door flowed like lava, pouring in its quiet heart of fire. The small, redwood deck beyond the door jutted out toward an ocean that was more alert than usual for that time of day, defying its tranquil name with healthy swells. Foam formed fingers determined to hold on, hold on, hold on, clutching at straws of sand and air, shells and shiny stones. First light faded out a blue moon.

Tanner Blue's birth certificate was laid out on a low, unfinished oak table beside her bed. The night before, she studied all the details feeling a necessary comfort in knowing that they were still faithful to the beginning of her life. Her name remained Tanner Blue Baptiste. She was born in Oakland, California, thirty years ago. June twenty-first, same day as her namesake, Henry Ossawa Tanner—the painter.

The custom-made Plexiglas bookcase left of the sliding door still belonged. The oak dresser against the north wall still matched the table beside her bed. The pine closet door beside her full bath in the southwest corner still needed refinishing. The 4×4-foot lithograph of abstract shapes—cool blues and warm reds—promised to step aside for some of her own original work.

"Tannerblue, what's wrong? Bad dream?"

She shuddered. Stood back from Nile and grasped his shoulders. "Nile—I just remembered being born!"

He shook his head. "That must have been some dream."

"I don't dream anymore, Nile."

"You don't remember."

"I do remember. That's why I stopped dreaming."

The room brightened and the words, *"Dado a luz,"* slipped from Tanner Blue's lips.

Nile tilted his head to one side. "Spanish?"

Slowly, Tanner Blue nodded. "I got straight A's. It means given to the light—being born, like a new day."

The doorbell buzzed and the phone rang, both shrill as sirens. Tanner Blue clutched her chest and Nile uttered a profound, "Be right back," before gravitating toward the front door.

On the third ring, Tanner Blue answered the black, cordless phone on the floor beside her bed.

"Happy birthday, Tan!"

"Kali...."

Tanner Blue met her best friend, Kalina, in middle school. Geography class in public school. They sat together in the third row, off to the left side of the room by a long row of windows that watched over Lake Merritt. Their teacher, Mr. Anders, told them to be quiet so he could take attendance.

"Tanner Blue Baptiste?"

Her arm shot in the air. "Present!"

Kalina leaned over and whispered to her, "I bet I'm next!"

"Kalina Buya?"

"Here." She raised and lowered her hand quickly.

Tanner Blue whispered. "Does it mean something?"

"What?"

"Your name."

"Uh huh."

"Tell me!" Tanner Blue squirmed.

"It was my father's idea."

"Papi named me too, after a famous painter."

"Papi?"

"Puerto Rican kids call their fathers that in New York, where Papi's from."

"He's Puerto Rican?"

Tanner Blue shook her head then shrugged. "I just started calling him that. It makes him happy."

"My name's *Taíno*."

"What's that?"

"Old people and an old language. *Kalina* means 'the Carib people' and *Buya* means 'good spirit.'"

"Why'd he name you after old people?"

Kalina giggled. "I mean the Caribs have been around a long time."

"You two girls. Stop talking."

They sank down in their seats and waited until Mr. Anders called a few more names. Tanner Blue surreptitiously tore a page from her black-and-white composition book, folded the blue-ruled sheet in half, and carefully tore it in two. Then, she scribbled a note.

Caribs. Is that the same as the Caribbean? My mother's from there. Antilla.

Kalina wrote on the other side of the scrap.

I think so. My mother and father are from Dominica. It's one of those islands.

You ever been there?

Nope.

I've never been to Antilla. I don't want to.

Me neither. I mean Dominica.

"Young ladies! Stop writing those notes."

They sat up straight. Looked away from each other for a few seconds. Then, they both folded their arms on their desks. Rested their chins on them.

Tanner Blue whispered, "Don't your parents want to go back sometime?"

"My mother says my father chose his 'people' over us so he's still back there and we're still here."

"My mother says she wants to go back 'home' when she has enough money. I don't want to go because...."

"Because why, Tanner Blue?"

"I don't know. The people might be mean."

"I like your name, Tanner Blue."

"I like yours too, Kalina."

"So, Blue's your middle name?"

"I guess."

"Wish I had one. Why'd he give you such a different name, though?"

"The painter. He said I'd understand better when I was grown up."

"I know what I want to be when I grow up. An interpreter. I just learned that word last week in this book about Native Americans."

"Kalina, how do you know?"

"Know what?"

"Who you want to be?"

"I want to be able to talk to my father."

"He doesn't speak English?"

"My mother says he doesn't like to, so I want to learn *Taíno*. What do you want to be when you grow up, Tanner Blue?"

"Wise. I always want to know what to do."

Mr. Anders clapped his hands. "Kalina Buya! Tanner Blue Baptiste! How'd you both like to meet the principal the first day of school?"

Tanner Blue looked toward the windows and Kalina's eyes wandered to the large bulletin board on a wall to the right.

As soon as Mr. Anders turned his back to write on the blackboard, the girls started scribbling new notes. Tanner Blue took a long time on one in particular, shaping block letters and using her new set of thin-tipped magic markers to color in background designs. Finally, she slid it to her new friend.

I like to make pictures.

"Wow!"

The teacher stared at Kalina, who quickly covered Tanner Blue's note with both hands. Then she wrote one of her own.

You should be an artist!

Reading those words, Tanner Blue's hands trembled. Her eyes stung when she blinked. Kalina mouthed, "What's wrong?"

"Nothing." Tanner Blue's voice cracked. She rubbed her eyes, trying to wipe away a month-old memory.

Twenty-one years shuffled by like a deftly handled deck of cards, and the mere sound of Kalina's voice amplified the power of their history. Tanner Blue could always count on that voice to remind her that she, herself, mattered. The two friends talked less often with each fleeting year, but as long as their voices could find each other, they could listen. As long as they could listen, especially to the volumes spoken between the lines, they would always be best friends.

"Tan, what's wrong?"

"You're the second one to ask me that today and it's not even…what time is it, Kali?"

"Something after nine o'clock, New York time."

"Hold on a minute." Tanner Blue tossed the phone on her bed, clutched at her birth certificate, and studied box 5a. She looked at the analog clock on the table that was level with her down pillow.

"Kali…"

"Tan?"

"I was being born, right now—6:17."

"You sound so strange, Tan. If you hadn't said my name when you answered the phone, I would've thought I had the wrong number. You feeling alright?"

While closing her door, Tanner Blue noticed that Nile was talking to someone at the threshold in the living room.

"Tan?"

"Sorry. I'm just waking up. I mean, I'm just realizing something."

"What?"

"There's so much we don't know, Kali. What if there's a way, a place, where we could start our lives all over again—have a second chance?"

"Everywhere's been discovered, Tan. Remember? Mr. Anders taught us that in geography. Hmm. He sure was fine."

"Yes, he was, but Kali, think about it—we wouldn't know if some place got overlooked unless, somehow, the people there wanted us to know and found a way to tell us how to get there."

"I'm sticking with what I learned in school, Tan. Besides, I don't need to start all over. I've never had more of what I want."

"What aren't you telling me, Kali? You're always reaching for something."

"They offered me a full-time job teaching English at Gunther High."

"Kali!!! I'm *so* happy for you!"

"You always told me the subbing and all those part-time jobs would add up to what I wanted. I was getting so tired, I couldn't see it anymore, Tan, but you did. I got *this* close to applying for an administration job when the teaching gig finally came through. I just wish…"

"What?"

"You still running the interlibrary loans office at the college?"

"Uh huh. Just got a raise."

"That's great, Tan. Congratulations! Wouldn't this be a good time to go back to school? You could get your degree by the end of next year. Tuition reimbursement is still one of your benefits, right?"

"Kali, not today."

"Tan, you know the happiest I've ever seen you?"

"Kali…"

"When you had that job in high school—the one where you designed paper towels at that factory."

"That was my first job. I was excited about working and making my own money. It could have been anything."

"But it wasn't anything, Tan. And there was something else you wanted to do..."

"Matching tissue boxes."

"That's right! Plenty of companies are using your ideas."

"It was just a pattern of silly squares."

"I always tell students how important it is to complete things, Tan. At thirty, it won't be getting any easier, you know?"

"I'm not one of your students."

The phone line went dead, not from hanging up—from hanging on.

"You celebrating?"

"I'm taking next week off. Think I'll just stay home for a change and enjoy being where I am."

"You're still happy way up there, with all those trees and all that water? All those people who look nothing like you or me?"

"Forget the people, Kali. There's something about this place— the mist, those redwoods you still haven't seen. The sound of the waves, the colors of the sky and water."

"Too much rain, Tan."

"But when it's clear and warm, Kali, and dry, it feels more magnificent than you could possibly imagine."

"Listen, I sent you something for your birthday. You didn't get it?"

"Mail's slow up here sometimes."

"Damn! It should have gotten to you by now."

"What is it?"

"I'm not exactly sure. I bought it from this woman I'd never seen before in the Village. I passed her table and got halfway down the steps to the subway but something called me back even though I was running late for work. She just showed me this thing, your present, and I knew you had to have it. The woman didn't say a word and I haven't seen her since. It's almost like she *made* me buy it."

"Now you *have* to tell me!"

"You always used to be the patient one. I do have some more news to tide you over. I can't believe I've held it in this long."

"Tell me!"

"This is *your* day, Tan, not mine."

"Then I say, whatever it is, tell me!"

"Guess."

"Kalina — don't mess with me."

"Victor asked me to marry him!"

"Wow."

"That all you have to say?"

"No, no. When?"

"Yesterday. I wanted to call you right away but I wanted to wait for your birthday more."

"I mean, when are you getting married?"

"I don't know yet but you'll have to come!"

"Wow, Kali. Of course, I'll come."

"Why don't you sound happy for me, Tan?"

"It's coming out of the blue."

"You're jealous."

"Don't tell me how I feel!"

"You *sound* jealous."

"Of what?"

"Relationships. You've locked yourself way up in the middle of nowhere so you don't have to deal with anyone else."

"Kali, even you don't *know* me."

"There are things I don't understand about you, Tan, but they don't stop me from caring, from being your best friend no matter what. After all these years, I still wonder, what will it take for you to live in *this* world?"

The phone line sighed, thinly connecting coast to coast, past to present, birth to life.

"Have you told your mother yet?"

"I'm taking my time with that. She never got over my father even though she left him. You know how protective she is."

"Protective...."

"Tan...?"

"Hmm?"

"Listen, I have to get ready. We're going to tell Victor's parents our news. I want you to be happy, Tan. Happy birthday. My *Taíno* blood tells me this will be a powerful time for you."

"Congratulations to you, Kali, and Victor. Tell him I said he's a very lucky man."

Tanner Blue hung up the phone, deserted by the receiver. Embers of memories smoldered in all four corners of the room. Drowning recollections conspired with the *Wave* to drag her out to sea and test whether she would sink, swim, or float. Riding waves, her instincts kicked, screamed, and pounded their fists against heavy air and forced Tanner Blue's head above the depths where once again, she could breathe.

"Tannerblue." Nile rapped three times at her bedroom door. "You okay in there?"

She followed the trail of his voice and pressed her cheek against the door. "I'm fine. Thanks. I just woke up kind of hard. That's all."

"That's all?"

"Uh, huh."

"The mail carrier messed up again. The neighbors brought over a package for you. A couple of cards, too. They're right here outside your door."

She listened for the reversal of his footsteps but he stood still.

"If you can remember being born, Tannerblue, you can do anything."

She placed a hand on the doorknob. "Nile?"

"Hmm?"

"You can, too."

"Remember being born or do anything?"

"Yes." She laughed.

"Hmm. Listen, if it's today, happy birthday."

The sound she waited for came. His footsteps retreated from her door leaving behind quiet without peace.

Tanner Blue returned to her bed and curled up in the fetal position, certain of two things: her father welcomed her birth heartily and her mother thought of it as labor.

Armande Baptiste grew up on 151st and Amsterdam in Harlem. He was tall and handsome in a gangly way. His slightly pock-marked skin was sensitive to razors though he stayed clean shaven as soon as facial hair appeared when he was just a teen. He trimmed his own hair faithfully every three weeks. A Puerto Rican girlfriend in high school nicknamed him *Canela*, Spanish for cinnamon, to celebrate the matching colors of their skin.

As a tender man, Armande meant to attend college and graduate with a degree. He tried hard to work toward it while in high school even though he had no parent, relative, neighbor, or friend who could show him the way. No guidance counselor ever took him aside to help direct his inborn skills. This was true even though every teacher observed the intensity of Armande's attention span no matter what task was set before him. His parents and their friends went to work and came home. They played cards and pic-nicked on weekends, their steady conversation tainted by infinite complaints. As a seen-not-heard child, Armande longed to ask his elders, "Don't any of you ever pick up a travel magazine or feel curi-ous about some foreign place in a movie?" Armande did both and wanted to do much more once he started making his own money.

A notice for his first job was posted on a bulletin board in the school library. A helper was needed at a bookbindery in Lower Man-hattan. The excursion downtown for the interview was a big deal for Armande. He had high hopes of being hired and branching out from there, for the first time seeing his life as an open road. After arriving early for his appointment, he was shown just once how to set up a book for binding. The boss was impressed with his precision and told him to start the next day.

The first book Armande worked on was about Henry Ossawa Tanner who knew from age thirteen that he would be a painter. Reading on the sly at work, Armande began to wonder if the artist also knew that someday he would be considered great in Paris before recognition glinted in the country of his birth. Did Henry Tanner see himself as great? Was he driven by his *purpose*?

As Armande wondered about his own purpose one gloomy afternoon while on the job, his supervisor, the boss's son, snatched the book about Henry Tanner from Armande's hands. After flipping through the text-heavy pages, stopping only at color plates, the demi-boss shut the book and remarked, "Why so much fuss about a nigger painter?" He tossed the book aside and waited impatiently for an answer.

Armande said, "Maybe you should read the whole book."

The reddened superior replied, "Maybe I should fire you."

"You didn't hire me."

"You're smart. You know whose side my old man will take."

Armande looked at the self-portrait of Henry Ossawa Tanner on the cover of the abandoned book. He swore he saw the painter's lips move, felt him place words in his own mouth, and before he knew it, Armande said, "I don't have to work for you." He could never get the rest of the details straight for exactly what followed. Armande knew he left with a final paycheck in his hand, and he wound up with two copies of the book that cost him his job but bought him his first taste of personal power. The part he simply could not recall was the look in the father's eyes—whether it was embarrassment, contempt, or some relative of regret. What Armande resented most was the interruption of his thoughts about purpose. Many times, he tried to pick up where he left off but it was as if a brick wall went up as soon as he raised the question. Each time, the wall got higher, its presence vaster, demanding more energy to scale. The fatigue of getting boxed in became far too great.

For five years after finishing high school, Armande rented a rundown apartment on the Lower East Side. In that time, he gradually disposed of the dream to go away to college as if it were a greasy bag fit only for the trash. Instead, he worked in cafés and offices, drove delivery trucks and limousines, and finally, managed a temporary employment agency. Then, one Saturday, he went to a matinée of *Porgy and Bess* in the West Village. It was summertime. Walking home, the transformation between west and east, with Fifth Avenue driven like a stake through the heart of both directions, magnified how far he had drifted from discovering his purpose. As he turned his corner, the lives of young men and women decorating the fronts of grocery stores seemed far smaller than the life he meant to lead. Already, he was twenty-three.

Unable to sleep that night, Armande became obsessed with leaving, aware that he would waste away completely by waiting a minute too long to make that move. One week later, he bought a sixty-dollar Greyhound Ameripass. Decided to go as far as he could imagine, to make the most of his ticket. He purchased a duffel bag from the Army-Navy store on 2nd Avenue and East 13th and within a month, he rode the bus all the way to Oakland, California, often wondering about Porgy's progress back to Bess. In those three-and-a-half days, the West Coast became as good a place as any to give his emerging dream a chance of coming true—a house and family all his own.

The house came first, thanks to Stone. Armande exchanged the universal *brother-nod* with him while they waited in line for lunch at the local cooking school one midweek day. It made Armande feel good to support the students as they practiced on the public. Plus, the food there was often good and always cheap. In the course of picking and choosing from the buffet, he dropped a fork that landed beside the sturdy work boot laced onto Stone's left foot. The moment after Armande said, "Nice boots," he wished he had not because his own were so shabby. Stone noticed that wear and tear. Paid for both their meals, which they shared in the dimly lit, airy cafeteria that looked out onto the Oakland estuary. A tall, blue-black-man built like his name, Stone listened more than he talked. When they stood up to discard their empty plates, he said to Armande, "I build houses, man. Maybe you could use some extra work."

It took three years but with Stone's help, Armande finished off a fixer-upper all his own primarily from scraps. He found a good location between downtown Oakland and Lake Merritt with a shy view of the water. That strong sense of completion inspired him to get serious about finding a woman to help make his house a home.

Summer weather trespassed on late October when Armande asked Marguerite Hadley to dance at a calypso party in San Francisco. He was twenty-six by then and she was twenty-four. On the way to the dance floor, she stopped to whisper in his ear, "I'm not too dark for you?" Any kind of dancing took some effort for Armande and this woman's words, somewhere between a directive and a question, ruined his rhythm before he could attempt a first step. He looked closely at her smooth, oval, pretty face and told her, "You have beautiful skin." He was inches taller and immediately wanted to do something that could lift her up.

Armande and Marguerite danced and laughed as she tried her best to show him how to move his hips back and forth, in and out in smooth circles. He soon gave up trying to follow everyone else's formula, inventing his own sway. Words overlaid their steps, causing them to discover that they both grew up in Harlem about ten blocks apart. An invitation from an older, female cousin living in San Francisco imported Marguerite from New York four years earlier. The two women worked as tellers at a major bank.

Over the next few months, Armande invited Marguerite on walks along the Oakland estuary, around Lake Merritt, beside the Berkeley Marina—flat places he thought friendly to shoes with high heels. She did not resist when he finally kissed her one Sunday outside the Grand Lake theatre where they had just taken in an evening showing of *Carmen Jones*. Marguerite said, "Yes," when Armande asked her if she wanted to see where he lived. She boldly followed him through the doorway to his tidy bedroom. Shook her head when he asked, "Mind if I close the door?"

He desired to take his time with her but she was more starved for touch than any woman he had ever known or dreamed of. If only he could have offered love on top of his own quiet hunger. Most of all, Armande wanted to eradicate the bitter root of her words, *I'm not too dark for you?*, hoping it was not buried far too deep for him to reach.

In the darkness of his bedroom, Armande turned toward Marguerite. Took her face in his constructive hands. She turned away. He turned on the light.

"No!" She jumped up to restore the darkness. He stood beside her at the wall switch. Covered her in the yellow chenille spread, their witness that possessed powers to reveal the roots of truth.

"Margie, I think you're beautiful."

"Even after…?"

"Yes, even after making love with you."

"I don't believe it." She flopped down on the side of the bed. Pulled the spread tightly around her shoulders.

"If you stick with me, you'll see I'm no liar."

"All men are the same."

He laughed. Sat down beside her. "I know that's what some mothers say but why do *you* say that, Margie? Look in my eyes and tell the truth." Armande waited patiently until her eyes finally found his.

"Would you put on some clothes first, Armande?"

He shook his head. "Tell me your *naked* truth."

"Don't think you're my first."

"I can tell I'm not."

"Well, he was black as me."

"Was he handsome?"

"Yes."

Armande laughed. "More than me?"

A brief smile teased the corners of Marguerite's mouth. "About the same."

"Right, because all men are the same."

"You only *think* you want me to be honest."

She got up. Walked over to the window. Sat on its ledge and bit her lip. Armande joined her. Placed firm hands on her slouching shoulders. Helped her sit up straight.

"He said I was too dark for him—too black."

"I'm not him, Margie."

"You're much lighter. You'll do me worse."

"Why would you even think or say that? Have I mistreated you?"

She shook her head. "Something my mother told me."

"And you believe it, whatever that was?"

"Yes, and you will, too."

They spent the next five Sunday afternoons together, walking, talking, making love. On the sixth, Armande was not shocked when Marguerite announced, "I'm pregnant." He asked calmly, "Do you want to get married?" She shrugged and said, "I don't care." Within the week, they became husband and wife with the lukewarm blessings of a novice preacher and his nervous spouse.

Loving anyone was troublesome for Marguerite Hadley—herself without escape. Her mother always said, "Margie, if you don't learn to bite that sharp tongue of yours, you won't be liked." Marguerite never learned but she did make one significant exception. In her heart of hearts, she regretted having had a child but never said as much.

Like her parents, Marguerite was born in Antilla. Unlike them, she did not grow up there. They moved to Harlem within a year of Marguerite's birth, as soon as her mother could withstand the long journey on an ocean liner. That passage had been endured by relatives before them who had staked out apartments in Manhattan's black haven. Marguerite's birth was inadequate, so after eight long years, her mother finally conceived a second time, delivering a son, Angelo, who arrived stillborn. He was memorialized in the photograph her father snapped with the consent of a sorrowful delivery-room nurse who had suffered three miscarriages in five years. That picture of the blue-skinned baby dominated the top of an antique player piano abandoned by former tenants who left in too much haste. Resistant to tuning, the clumsy instrument imposed itself in a dark and dusty corner of the small Harlem living room. Its shadows held happiness for ransom the twenty years Marguerite lived in that apartment. A pact between the piano and Angelo gave him eyes that watched Marguerite relentlessly through tight-closed lids. The piano and fetus shared a sense of disposal composed by unplayed music that was felt instead of heard. Marguerite trained herself not to look at those collaborations even though daily, she had to pass through the living room to reach the bath from the small cubby where she slept. Through their father, Angelo blamed her for being a survivor.

Despite the fetus turning up blue, Reginald Hadley swore to family, acquaintances, and strangers that his son, Angelo, would have passed for white—a wish far unfulfilled by his own pigmentation. Unlike the daughter, the son was crowned with a head full of good hair. Though high yellow, his wife could not pass but she could have done better than to generate such a sooty, wrong-haired, plain-faced specimen in the daughter. And how many times did he have to tell both woman and child, "*She* was not supposed to be born."

Vaudine Hadley conceded that her dead baby was surely lighter than his sister, with better hair. Yet and still, both parents found creative ways to blame each other for the faulty conception in heated arguments each Friday night.

Growing up, Marguerite was clever enough not to blame herself for her parents' stubborn misery and unrelenting grief, or accept credit for the perverse comfort it provided them. However, in her own process of imitation, she matched the level of their overall dissatisfaction with life by avoiding any behavior that promoted healing.

If only Armande Baptiste had left her alone. Nothing but honest, she told him flat out the day they danced, "I'm too dark for you." Or had she asked him? Either way, it was his fault for not believing her. If only being too dark could have prevented her from getting pregnant.

In her semi-private recovery room, Marguerite refused her daughter when the nurse tried to place the cleaned up and inspected newborn in her arms. So, Armande was the first parent to know the baby with a touch. He felt like a magician, delicately balancing her warmth, shape, and weight in hands that built houses. It was nothing less than a miracle that those same two hands, ten fingers, could also hold exactly the kind of life that made his work worthwhile. Knowing that his blood flowed through her heart, he finally had no doubt about what it meant to love. She was so small and trusting in his hands but not helpless. Immediately, he felt her strength. At that moment, his whole world weighed six pounds and eight ounces. Pacing back and forth, he thought about the room he had prepared for the arrival of his child—building her crib, changing table, and dresser. Blending heart and soul into the custom blue paint he mixed up for the walls. Peering briefly out the window of the recovery room into a hazy dawn, all he saw was bright sunshine and the bluest skies.

Armande kissed every inch of his daughter's face and focused on her clenched eyelids.

"Margie, did you see that? She just winked at me!"

"You're tired, man. Been here the whole time. Why don't you just go home?"

He focused on his child.

"Nothing could keep me from this, *Tanner Blue*. I *saw* you wink at me! I saw you come into this world." Armande Baptiste's eyes grew full like his entire soul.

"What did you just call her?"

"Her name."

"No, I told you, nothing blue. And please, Armande, *please* don't tell me about that damn painter again."

He turned to his wife.

"Look, Margie. She's smiling at you!"

"You're always seeing things."

"You're not going to believe this, Margie. You know what day it is?"

"Armande, *please*, just let me rest."

Holding his daughter securely in the crook of one arm, with the other, he touched Marguerite's shoulder and sat gently on the side of her bed.

"Henry Tanner was born on this same day—June twenty-first."

Slowly, Marguerite inched up. "The start of summer?" She brightened, briefly.

"I hadn't even thought of that! Yes, this is the first full day. See, Margie? The name, it's perfect. Everything will be perfect. There's so much I want to do, Margie. There's so much I *can* do. What do you think...just listen to this: I want to start painting designs on peoples' front doors—something special, something that makes a person feel right at home even before they go inside. I know I get carried away with Henry Tanner but he was a great man, Margie. So great, the French named a color after him."

"Come now, Armande. I've never known anyone great, have you?"

He nodded and forced Tanner Blue into her mother's ashen arms.

~2~

The idea was an arrow aimed at celebration a month before Tanner Blue's high-school graduation. Neither parent had said anything about a party or special dinner, nor asked her if she wanted some reasonable gift. Finally, one Saturday afternoon, Tanner Blue's patience left her like a slave redirected by its own North Star. The Baptiste family was sitting silently in their living room where Tanner Blue pretended to read a short story in the corduroy, rust-colored chair by the window. Lake Merritt dominated her attention from the corner of her eye and she wished to attract the calmness it infused in the runners, walkers, and drivers caught up in its watery orbit. Cream, lace curtains danced to music on the gentle breeze that blew in from the quiet street. Early afternoon sun brightened the gray-green walls that felt like cold rain during long winter months. Pine, hardwood floors glowed beneath the large circle topped by a new woolen carpet—blue with flecks of rust.

Through headphones, Armande listened to the private jazz collection he had recorded, patting his foot, his gaze intersecting Tanner Blue's as he looked out her window, far beyond the lake. From the velour, forest-green sofa, Marguerite stared in the general direction of the animated television, muttering regularly about how its programs were a royal waste of time.

Tanner Blue put down her book and sat on the arm of her father's chair, the same family as hers but gray. The mismatched furniture was growing old, like the fierce, recurring argument her parents had about the colliding colors, styles, and fabrics until they recently became aware of Tanner Blue as their constant witness. On occasion, her presence could cause them both to forfeit that omnipotent last word when it was overpowered by the slightest twinge of conscience.

Armande took off his headphones and stroked Tanner Blue's chin.

"Only thirty more days to graduation, Papi."

"You excited, Blue?"

She shook her head. "I don't even really want to go to graduation but I was wondering. Could we go to Shells on the Bay? Us and Kali—and her mom?"

"Shells in Berkeley?" Marguerite sat up straight. "It's too expensive."

"I've saved some money."

"Child, you'd better save it. You must learn to take care of yourself."

"Margie. This is a very special occasion. Yes, Blue. We can go to Shells."

Marguerite sat up straighter. "Armande, didn't you just hear what I said? Of course you did. You always do but it makes no matter."

"That's okay, Papi. It was just an idea." Tanner Blue swung her foot back and forth, kicking the side of her father's chair.

"Stop that! You're ruining the furniture." Marguerite pointed at the chair.

Tanner Blue could not stop.

"No, Margie. You stop it. Stop thinking of yourself."

Marguerite stiffened. "*Myself*? Why don't *you* tell me what it's like to be selfish?"

Armande took a deep breath. "Listen, Margie, can't we just make it through graduation?"

Foot still swinging, Tanner Blue stared at her father. "What happens after graduation, Papi?"

Armande cleared his throat. "You go to the community college, Blue. That's what."

Tanner Blue shook her head. "You meant something else."

Marguerite relaxed her spine a bit. "Well, at least we didn't raise a fool."

"Margie, why don't you just relax."

"Impossible in this house."

"I'll just make believe I didn't say anything." Tanner Blue went back to her chair, picked up her book, and turned it right-side up.

"Life isn't like that, child. One way or another, you have to finish what you start."

"I don't want to finish it, M." Tanner Blue stared at her book, the words a foreign language.

"M. You won't even call me *mother* or *mom* like a normal child."

"Don't you remember *why*?"

"You think you're a grown, grown woman, do you? Like you can handle anything just so." Marguerite snapped her fingers like lightning.

Tanner Blue folded her arms across her chest. "I'll always remember because I can't forget."

"Blue. Please, don't let that ruin your life. I know what words can do."

"Nothing's going to ruin my life, Papi." She turned toward her mother. "No one."

"Then, child, let me tell you something."

"Margie."

"Man, there's no point in waiting."

"Don't do this, Margie." Armande twisted in his daughter's direction. "Blue, I'll take you to Shells. We can go right now and make our reservation." He took his daughter's arm, trying to get her to stand and walk away.

Tanner Blue sat firm. "M, what were you just talking about?"

"See what I mean, man? She's talking to me like she's a grown, grown woman."

"I'm just asking a simple question."

Marguerite gusted toward Tanner Blue and cracked her across the left cheek. "Who you calling, 'simple'?"

Armande squeezed Marguerite's wrist.

"That hurts!" Marguerite spoke but Tanner Blue felt the pain. "Your father and me, we're finally divorcing."

Marguerite's hand fell like rotted fruit from Armande's loosened grip.

"Good!" Tanner Blue pressed the back of her hand against her cheek.

"See, I told you she wouldn't even care."

"Blue, this is not how I wanted to tell you." Armande put his arm around her shoulder, then faced his wife. "Marguerite, it doesn't help to know why you're so evil."

"So you know me now, after all these years?"

"I've always known you. If only I'd known better...."

Tanner Blue stood up.

"Wait, Blue. I don't know what I'm saying. Neither does your mother."

Marguerite walked right up to him. "I'm tired of biting my tongue."

"That's one problem you never, ever had, Margie."

"How would you know? You stay so busy chasing all your worthless ideas."

"They're...not...worthless."

"Oh, I'm hurting your soft, soft feelings, again. What kind of man are you?"

"I've provided for my family. Margie, I don't have to answer to you but couldn't you have waited until Blue graduated?"

She shook her head. "Man, I got too tired."

Tanner Blue looked from one parent to the other. "What about our house? Where'm I going to live?"

Armande opened his mouth. Marguerite spoke.

"We're selling it. I'll give your father that." She looked around, nodding in approval. "This place was a very good investment."

"That's all it was to you?" Tanner Blue stared at her mother, trying not to hate.

"It has been a roof over our heads."

Tanner Blue looked at her father. "Papi, you *built* this house. You can't just sell it!"

"Blue, sometimes, in cases like this, it's best to get rid of the memories. Lucky for us, this is a seller's market, so, we just accepted a very high offer. I'll be able to send you to a fancier school after your first year and do some things I've been wanting to get to."

"Papi, I don't care about school. You don't have to take any offer!"

"It's too late, Blue. I can't tell you how much I wanted to ease into this but I'm close to buying a fixer upper over in Grass Valley, up the road from the zoo. You'll love it. You can live with me."

"Man, that's just another one of your senseless dreams."

"Margie, dreams aren't *supposed* to make sense. They're *supposed* to come true...."

Tanner Blue faded to her room without being asked or noticed, no longer as a child. She belonged completely to herself and the letter that lay on her desk. The letter promised a scholarship to Redwood State College way up north, along with a work-study job that started in summer.

She closed the door. Sat at her desk by the window and read the acceptance letter. Looked up every sentence or so to make sure her private view of the lake was still there, wary of the suddenness of change.

The last line of the letter read, "Respond by April 15th in order to guarantee your receipt of this scholarship."

No! That was three weeks ago!

Tanner Blue paced the length of her twin bed, which was covered with a blue batik spread. Rushed back to the letter, looking for a number to call and a name to ask for—Ms. Perla Magena, Director of Educational Opportunity Programs. Then, she remembered it was Saturday.

I'll call anyway and leave a message. I'll call back first thing Monday morning. They have to let me in!

She rehearsed in her mind what to say, determined not to beg, resolved to get what was hers. Tanner Blue dialed and waited for an answering machine to come on.

"Hello?" A woman answered on the first ring.

"Oh!"

"Hellooo."

"Excuse me. Is this Ms. Magena?"

"Yes."

"You're working on a Saturday?"

"Who's calling?"

"Sorry. This is Tanner Blue Baptiste. I'm calling about my scholarship."

"*Your* scholarship?"

"Yes, I have a letter."

"You know the deadline has passed."

"Yeah, I was just reading about that." Tanner Blue took a deep breath. "I need another chance."

"I'm afraid you missed your chance."

"Isn't this still really the same chance? I mean, the letter also says orientation starts on June 15th and lasts until school starts at the end of August. There's still time."

"That's not how it works. We have a long waiting list, so when scholarship recipients don't meet the deadlines, we have to give ourselves enough time to fill those slots."

"Are all the slots filled?"

"We're still notifying some alternates. That's what I'm doing here on a Saturday."

"Your list, is it alphabetical?"

"We have a ranking system."

"Well, if there are slots open, and I was an original recipient, shouldn't I still be entitled to my slot?"

"Tell me, Tanner Blue, why did you miss the deadline and why are you so determined to accept the scholarship now?"

Tanner Blue stood still, hoping it would help her think more clearly on her feet.

"It's hard to say."

"Tell me the truth."

Tanner Blue gnawed at her upper lip. "Problems at home."

"I see. Have you thought about a major?"

"You mean the scholarship's still mine?"

"That's not what I said."

"No, I haven't thought about it."

"You should have."

"I've given you an honest answer."

"What's your favorite subject?"

"It's hard to say."

"You got A's in foreign languages and art these past two years."

"Art is like a foreign language. You have to *think* in it if you really want to speak it. You have to let yourself get lost."

"You can do all that?"

Tanner Blue shrugged. "It was easier for me to get good grades than bad ones, so I did."

"I take my work seriously, Tanner Blue. You're one of the most interesting people I've talked with in a while."

Interesting?

"Ms. Magena, I *really* want to come to your school."

"This is a very isolated part of the state, you know. No diversity to speak of."

"I'm used to that in schools."

"Would this be your first time away from home?"

Tanner Blue nodded, then said, "Yes. But...."

"But what?"

"Soon, I won't have a home."

"I see. Then let me say this. Don't think you'd be able to run away from anything by coming here. The only reason to make a move like this is to get an education. No matter what's going on, you can never fool yourself for very long."

"I'm telling you the truth, Ms. Magena. I need to get away *and* I want an education. I can go to the community college, I'm all registered, but if I have this opportunity, I don't want to regret letting it get away from me."

"That's a very mature way to look at it."

Patience, Tanner Blue. Patience.

"Hold on a minute, young lady. Let me check something."

In that minute, Tanner Blue watched the clock, checked the watch in her jewelry box several times, and swore she saw the sun sink closer to the horizon. Finally, Ms. Magena got back on the line.

"Still there?"

"Yes."

"I had to do some thinking."

Patience, Tanner Blue.

"More than anything else, I tend to trust my instincts, dear."

Dear?

"I can make room for you but only if you promise me two things."

Tanner Blue's hands trembled. "I won't disappoint you."

"It's not that."

"Please tell me."

"Finish what you start. Will you do that?"

The echo of her mother's words rippled in her ears like a tidal wave. She did not want to lie either by saying 'yes' when she knew 'no' was a strong possibility, or by being less than direct. So, she bit her tongue and rode the echo's last wave.

"Yes, one way or another, I will. What's the other thing?"

"I read this article lately about how we all know what we're supposed to do with our lives when we're nine years old. Imagine that. Some of us stick with it but most of us don't even remember what that thing might have been. I want you to remember, Tanner Blue, and I want you to stick with it."

"I have a good memory, Ms. Magena. I'll do my best."

"Well then. Without having met you yet, that's good enough for now. Get that acceptance letter in the mail to me no later than Monday. Send it overnight delivery."

For the first time in her life, Tanner Blue felt weary. The words, "Thank you," exploded from somewhere deep inside her soul. They were fireworks lighting the way to a whole new world.

"I'm sorry for this mess, kiddo." Armande stood beside his daughter at the desk he made for her when she turned ten. Placed a shaky hand on her left shoulder. "Those Greeks or Romans—whoever they were—knew what they were doing when they came up with apologies. There are times when, well, that's all anyone can do."

Tanner Blue wanted to cry but could not. She had never seen her mother shed a tear. Her father's eyes were the ones that welled up on occasion, like then.

"You know, Blue, when things don't work out, kids can blame themselves and it's never their fault. No matter how it looks, baby, you have to know how much I *wanted* to have you."

Tanner Blue's spine grew tense. "I know, Papi."

He noticed the paper on the desk and cleared his throat. "What's that?"

"I got a scholarship."

"Let me see it."

She handed him the letter. He read, slowly, ending with a sad smile. "You want to go all the way up there by yourself?"

"Yes."

"What about college here?"

"That was before."

Armande sat heavily on the side of Tanner Blue's bed, right next to her desk. Leaned over, resting elbows on his knees.

"I remember leaving home, Blue."

Tanner Blue studied her father. He had always looked younger than his years but that day, he looked closer to sixty than any forty-two.

"Ever wish you'd stayed in New York?"

Armande visited that same place way past the lake but returned more serenely this time. Shook his head and placed his hands on his knees. Took his time standing.

"Your back's bothering you again, Papi."

"It's nothing, kiddo." Upright, he winced briefly before bending forward just enough to hold his daughter's face in his roughened hands. "You sure you want to go? Our new house is pretty nice the way it is and, you know me, I've got plenty of plans for it."

"I have to go, Papi. I missed the deadline but I got them to make an exception. I gave them my word. I got that from you."

"You'll make mistakes, baby. I'm not saying this is one of them but only get into things you can get out of, and you'll be alright. Remember, you'll always have everything you need. You'll get

~38~

a lot of what you want. Then, all you have to know is what to do with it."

"How do you know these things, Papi?"

"I named you. I knew you before you were born." He kissed her on the forehead. Straightened up, hands pressed to his lower back. "I could use a walk. Want to come?"

Tanner Blue looked from her paperwork to her father.

"I'd better take care of this."

"Let me know if you need some help, a signature or something."

Jumping up and catching her father around the waist, Tanner Blue hugged him hard. Rested her head on his chest. Then, she gently let him go.

Marguerite stood in the doorway. "I have some good news for you, child."

"I've had enough for one day."

"Slapping you does no good. I'm going back home."

"*Home?*"

"Antilla. I've got people there starting up a real estate business. They want me to come help them." She pulled a letter from her gray house dress, fanning the air with the wrinkled aerogramme. "They *need* me to help them. All those years as a loan officer are paying off. You and your father, you'll finally be rid of me."

"No."

"Beg pardon?"

"I won't be living with Papi."

"I know you don't want to come with me."

"You're right."

"Then, what you mean, '*No*'?"

"I'm going away to school. I got a scholarship."

"Why this is the first I'm hearing of it? Your father knew?"

"I put it out of my mind, until today."

"Where?"

"The North Coast."

"*North Coast* of where?"

"California."

"They paying for everything?"

"Yes, plus a job."

"You trust some strangers?" Marguerite's gaze roamed to the letter. "Let me see that."

Tanner Blue sat still. Moved aside to avoid her mother's touch as she grabbed the letter.

"You missed the deadline."

"They're giving me a second chance."

"Child, you don't know how lucky you are."

"Right. How many other seniors have their parents get divorced a month before graduation?" Tanner Blue stared and stared, trying to see M as having once been a child. She could not do it.

"I've been under a lot of pressure, child. Work, your father, the people back home."

"Am I on that list?"

"You just don't understand."

"Understand what?"

"You always ask too many questions."

"I'll pack them up and take them with me."

"Watch your mouth. You still have some days under this roof with me. You think this is a joke?"

"No, M."

"You think I don't remember when that started, child? What you bring this up for now?"

"When did it start, M?"

"If you'd just call me *mother*...." Marguerite hugged herself hard to steady her hands and calm the tremor in her stomach.

"I was nine years old, M. I told you one of my teachers asked me what I wanted to be and I said an artist. I told you first, before Papi! I knew he'd understand but I wanted to give you a chance to understand me."

"Which teacher?"

"*Which teacher*? What difference...geography. Mr. Anders."

"What would he know about art?"

"That's not the point!"

"Tell me, then! What *is* the damn point?"

"What you said to me."

"I've said a lot of things. I guess they were the wrong ones."

"You've said things but we never talk."

"Like this—this is how you want to talk?"

"No, not like this. I want you to remember *what*, not just *when*."

"Child, would you just *tell* me? You've giving me a head-ache."

Tanner Blue got her mother a coated aspirin and a cool glass of water. It took Marguerite three tries to swallow the pill.

"Now, tell me what horrible thing I did to you. Or, should I just ask to be forgiven?"

"You said, '*Can't make money at that.*'"

"I was just being truthful! I'm your *mother*."

Tanner Blue let out a great sob. "Then *act* like it!"

"What have I been doing all these years? You've always had enough to eat. Nice clothes. A safe, comfortable place to live. Child, I've given you all I've got!"

Then, Tanner Blue knew her mother was telling the truth. "I know, I know, I know. Thank you. Mother."

Daughter looked at mother, pupil to pupil, each woman knowing there was nothing more to say.

~3~

Memories robbed Tanner Blue's room of oxygen like some haughty two-bit thief. She tore open the sliding glass door and bathroom window. Showered quickly, embracing air and water. Her thick aqua towel dried her skin until it was arid as earth and fire, ready to devour the French lavender lotion she smoothed along her arms and legs. The old blue jeans and white, cotton, long-sleeved blouse she plucked from her closet went on tighter than they did at twenty-nine. She could not bring herself to look in the mirror, fearful that its reflection would launch her into an oblivion from which she would be unable to return. Instead, she joined Nile in the dinette outside her bedroom door where he was juicing wheatgrass into a small glass decorated with red cherries.

"Hey, Tannerblue." He pointed his chin to the left of her door. A medium-sized package and two envelopes—blue on top of white—took up slight space on the floor.

She picked up the items. Walked toward Nile and placed them on the round, oak kitchen table.

"Want some?" He offered her some juice. "It's good for you." Nile placed the glass in her hand.

"Thank you."

He made himself some juice and they clinked glasses.

"You know, Tannerblue, birthdays are the only holidays I like to celebrate. Got any time for me today?"

She swirled the green foamy juice several times before taking a sip. "I'm on my way to the store."

"Buy yourself something special?"

"Food."

"Food? What about when you get back?"

"I'd like to do something peaceful and quiet."

"How about a nice, smooth walk on the beach? We've got that big old ocean right out there and all I do is neglect it."

Tanner Blue's gaze floated from the envelopes and package to meet the look on Nile's face—a glowing kindness that felt transferred from her father. Nile had suggested that they go shopping together several times and she always made an excuse. He had not asked lately and she missed the invitations. She looked out the window, which framed a living picture of the ocean.

"My father grew up in New York City and never went to the Statue of Liberty until I asked him to take me. When we made it to the top, he said, 'Blue, we do some things when we're ready.' Then, he shook his head and added, 'It can be so easy to look way past what's standing right in front of you.' He hugged me tight and looked me right in the eye. We stood there until a security guard asked us to keep moving."

Nile downed his wheatgrass juice and rinsed his glass in the sink. Turned toward Tanner Blue and smiled. "Maybe you'll be ready for that walk when you get back. Take your time. It's the longest day of the year."

"You need anything from Three Squares—some of that bread you like?"

"Yeah. Thanks." Nile reached in his pocket and pulled out a five.

"My treat."

"But it's *your* birthday."

"Then let me have my way." She took a bigger sip of the juice than before.

"Say now, aren't you curious about your package?" He nodded toward the table. "If it was mine, I would have opened it first thing."

Tanner Blue shrugged. "I know who it's from."

"But do you know what it is?"

"Not yet."

"I can't stand this! Can *I* open it?"

Tanner Blue laughed. "Nile, how do you always get to the mail first, I mean, even with the mix-ups at the post office?"

"I've always loved getting mail. I remember the very first letter someone sent me."

"Who was it from?"

"Come, sit just a minute. I'll tell you about it." He put his hand lightly on Tanner Blue's shoulder and eased her toward the leather, maroon sofa in the living room, where they sat on opposite ends. She pushed the glass coffee table out a few inches, crossed her legs, and rested her glass on her knee.

Nile turned toward Tanner Blue and folded an arm over the back of the couch.

"You ever have a pen pal?"

Tanner Blue shook her head.

"I grew up in Berkeley and had this pen pal, Freeson. He was from this black town in southeastern Canada. Can't think of the name of it right now. We wrote two letters a piece and that was it. Lasted about a year."

"Who stopped writing?"

"He did."

"How old were you?"

"Fifth grade. Ten."

Tanner Blue sank back into the sofa. "Papi took me to Allensworth once when I was nine."

"*Papi*? Daddy's girl?"

"More than you could know."

Nile rested his right ankle on top of his left knee. Leaned in Tanner Blue's direction. "Allensworth. I've passed the sign driving through the Central Valley."

"You know it was a black town?"

Nile shook his head. "Tell me about it."

"It lasted six years or so, in the early 1900s. The founder, Colonel Allensworth, was 'accidentally' run over twice and killed by a motorcyclist outside Los Angeles. Right around that time, arsenic was found in the town's water supply. That ruined the land and who knows how many people were poisoned."

"Damn, Tannerblue."

She uncrossed her legs and placed her glass on the coffee table.

"You know what has stayed with me the most about that history, Nile?"

"Tell me."

"I wasn't there but those people, they made their own town because they couldn't find a place that wanted them. They just wanted to be left alone. Why is that so hard? There's got to be a place like that."

"Tell you what, Tannerblue. When you find that place, do let me know."

"Thank you for that *when* and also for the juice." She drained her glass and placed it beside his in the sink.

"What about your mail?"

"I'll open it, later. See you."

She picked up the package and envelopes. Decided that the safest place for them was in the shed.

Magenta ice plants lined the short path that led from the back of the house to the weathered shed. Their petals were half open, waiting for just a little bit more warmth before unfolding completely. They swept down the cliff that led to the beach, tangling their magenta with bright, yellow mustard flowers perfumed by honeysuckle. The sun was still making up its mind about how much to shine, distracted by a bank of fog determined to win the daily contest.

The shed clung beside the top of a railed staircase that tumbled toward the shore. Tanner Blue handed the package and envelopes to a thick jade-and-aloe bush while she wrestled with the door's lock, which was as rusty as its key. Halfheartedly, she tried to open the door as more rust gathered around her memories of the last time she entered the shed, increasing the resistance. She forced the lock, overcome by the mustiness of memory. Surrendering, the back of the door hit the side of an old, stainless steel sink. Standing at the threshold, it was easy for Tanner Blue to pretend that she was seeing the inside of the shed for the first time.

She placed her cargo on the workbench that was nudged beneath a long windowsill fronting the ocean. An old jar of paintbrushes, dried-up tubes of acrylic paint, and an oval, paint-stained palette rested on the bench as comfortably as driftwood marking the beach. Rags stiffened by old paint were smothered in a plastic bag. In a corner, to the left of the workbench, a wooden easel was splattered with layers of cyan, Phthalo blue, and ultramarine paint. An oak bar stool was pushed off to the left side of the easel.

Something else was in that shed. Somethings. Tanner Blue felt their presence, resisting the challenge to try again to stare them down. The darkest corner held a stack of paintings that she preferred to think of as canvases. Canvases had potential.

Paintings are set in stone once you lay down layer after layer of paint and convince images to cover one another. After all that work, something in you always knows where it all began if you are willing to remember.

Hovering above the heap of paintings was a memory-cloud, solid as an icicle that wanted nothing more than to melt on that first day of summer.

Tanner Blue stared at all that negative space surrounding the heap. She looked so long, it became a physical thing—hard, sharp, burning.

Why didn't I just get rid of you when I had the chance?

She closed the shed door. Placed her right ear to it. Listened long enough to hear an answer.

You cannot throw away your soul.

Ocean, beach, and freeway were brush strokes that traced the North Coast of California. Turning tides changed colors—blue, green, lavender—reflecting on borrowed sunlight, resisting the pull of the full, daylight moon for as long as possible, which was not long at all. Games were the pastime of those tides, some a harmless ebb, others the ferocious tug of undertow.

Seabirds strutted the sand when they figured no enemies were watching. It was only when their skinny legs grew tired that they took to the sky, wearing out their wings. Floating on deep waters, they fished and ate until their beaks turned brittle. Pushed and pulled to repeat routines, they migrated here and there and here, again, seeking the warmest weather of all—that fiery place inside their souls.

Coasting south from Tourmaline Beach, Tanner Blue slowed down behind a green-and-white VW bus preparing for an incline that loomed ahead like Everest. She was no more, no less, than a black-woman in the blue car who had driven up and down that freeway week after week for the past twelve years.

Twelve years!

Tanner Blue shuddered, trying to steady her hands on the steering wheel. For the first time, she understood what it meant for time to fly.

The Three Squares market was a corner grocery store the first time Tanner Blue shopped there shortly after moving north. It tripled in size within its first five years and since, there were regular whispers of expansion. She was living on campus then, in a five-story dorm overlooking the freeway. Redwoods wove a halo around the complex, waving a heavy mist of spell-casting fog the longer you inhaled it. If you caught yourself holding your breath just once, you knew walking away would never be a simple act. In an instant, upside down became inside out and all that mattered was what was in your mind, not on it. Then, where would you be? Tanner Blue had asked herself that question many times, under her breath, meeting with an answer vowed to silence.

Three Squares was in walking distance from the dorm. Others in her orientation program did not notice when she went off on her own early in the afternoon that June twenty-first. The seven blocks see-sawed toward the town square past Victorians like ones her father had restored in different parts of the Bay Area. He was always so proud of his work, putting in a good day's worth of sweat. She slowed down in front of a few houses of different styles, imagining custom paintings on their front doors that her father could create according to his dream. She envisioned birds, plants, and stones— bright and multicolored. Had anyone baked her a cake and lit some candles for her eighteenth birthday, she would have wished that her father could live by doing the work he wanted most.

Despite the short distance and her youth, she was tired after reaching the square on foot before she owned a car. She picked up a free, local paper and sat on one of many benches in the midst of palm trees that looked so out of place in the moody climate, she wondered if they felt self-conscious. A few couples passed her by and they looked so happy, she wished she had a boyfriend. Dogs were popular on the square and she realized she did not have a favorite.

Tanner Blue read a few of the news stories about marijuana raids, the logging industry, and the new president of the college. Paid closer attention to the ads. There was one for the grand opening of a health food restaurant. Kalina's mother went vegetarian in their senior year. That is how tofu, wheatgrass, and soy milk came into Tanner Blue's life even though she still ate meat when it became a craving. The cross streets of the restaurant did not yet sound familiar. Looking up from the paper, she noticed the Rainy Days bookstore on the west side of the square. A white-man with curly, reddish hair stood outside smoking something. She got up and crossed the street to ask him about the restaurant. As she approached, the man put out his cigarette and went back inside the store. Tanner Blue walked in and showed him the ad in the paper.

"Hi. Would you tell me how to get there?"

"Sorry." The man shuffled some papers on the counter in front of him. He would not see her.

Tanner Blue's heart beat strong with rage and fear. "My father told me about you."

The man winced in her direction. "I don't know your father."

"*He* knows *you*. I'll find what I'm looking for."

She stormed outside into drizzle billowing toward heavy rain. Three Squares was doors away but what if it was filled with more people like the man in Rainy Days? She forgot to bring an umbrella and her fleece jacket was no match for the torrent. Under cover of awnings, she exchanged wet for dry, shopping slowly to give the rain a chance to lessen. Inside the store, Tanner Blue felt that everyone was watching her, waiting for her to take one thing she did not own. No one knew her. If they did, they would also realize her footsteps fit the mold of peace.

Clouds crushed sunlight as Tanner Blue drove past the green-and-white sign one mile from her exit. While signaling to turn off, she glanced briefly in the direction of the library where her corner office overlooked the other side of the freeway. Lately, she found herself drawn into the rhythm of north-south traffic outside her window, lost wondering about destinations. What were all those travelers leaving to arrive at some new place? What were they running to?

When she reached the plaza, a space opened up in front of the Three Squares market. As she parked and locked the door of her car, Tanner Blue noticed a man standing in front of Rainy Days books dragging on a cigarette. Its thin threads of smoke followed the lines of wrinkles in his face. His hair was thinned out, mostly gray, the rest, a faded red. Thick-lensed glasses rested on the bridge of his nose like blinders. She recognized him as the same man from twelve birthdays ago, and she had not set foot inside that store since. A colorful sign in the window announced a sale on children's books. The bright reds, yellows, and blues lured Tanner Blue closer. A small, plastic statue of a raven guarded the lower-left corner of the window.

"Smoke bother you?"

"It does." Tanner Blue fanned the air and stood beside the raven.

He flicked ashes to the ground. "Bad habit for a long time."

"Why'd you ask?"

"Never know who you're talking to these days." He crushed the butt with his right foot and went inside his store.

Walking slowly toward the corner market, Tanner Blue tried to decide whether she had just witnessed progress. The marshy nostalgia of the Bottoms that surrounded Three Squares held no answers for her. Glowing red beside the entrance to the store, an empty shopping cart waited, ready to wheel her forward.

Inside, a skylight did a remarkable job of keeping the market well lit, despite gray skies that rarely took a holiday. Maize colored walls collected brightness as workers in sky-blue aprons tended to the produce and customers. The Three Squares logo was a trio of scattered children's blocks—red, green, and blue on a banana-yellow background. This symbol was painted above gray, rubber doors that led to the stocking area at the back of the market.

Tanner Blue carefully chose *gai lan* greens, broccoli, and rainbow chard. She picked up an Indian eggplant and some heirloom tomatoes on the way to the fruit section. The store wasn't crowded yet, so she traveled with her cart instead of parking it off to the side somewhere and returning to it when her arms got full.

A handwritten sign said:

Cortland Apples

$1.00/lb-Crisp and Tart

Sliced samples filled a small plastic container beneath the sign. Tanner Blue stuck a toothpick into a piece of the firm fruit and took one small bite. It tasted like pie straight out of the oven. There were about nine other kinds of apples but Tanner Blue favored the Cortlands, choosing each apple for its color. Red streaks blended with tones of orange and yellow in an excitement of unpredictable patterns. Holding one in her left hand, she circled it with her right thumb. It was mostly smooth with just a little roughness, like the voice that called her name.

"Ms. Baptiste."

Tanner Blue smiled into a familiar face but could not recall the name. "Hello. Forgive me."

"Grace. You taught me how to read in your program at the library." She shifted her metal shopping basket from one hand to the other as if the salad greens, scallions, and green, plastic container of cherry tomatoes were many times their weight.

Tanner Blue bent slightly to hug that child who was around fourteen and heavier than Tanner Blue remembered. Mild acne layered her complexion, which was the color of nutmeg blended with cinnamon. Her natural black hair was brushed back into a small, neat bun. She wore a cantaloupe-colored sweater with cranberry trim and gray corduroy pants.

"So good to see you, Grace!" Tanner Blue released her. Let a hand rest on her shoulder for a moment before placing it on the bar of her shopping cart.

"Good to see you, too. I'm getting A's. I want to go to college."

"Then, that will be your destiny. Always remember how smart you are."

Grace held up her shopping basket. "I'm trying to eat right, too. This store's out of the way but I like to come here when I can, to get better food." She lowered her voice. "Sometimes, I stay away because I feel out of place."

Tanner Blue moved one step closer to Grace and said, "I know what you mean."

"Sorry to leave you by yourself, Ms. Baptiste, but I have to catch the bus in the next thirty minutes."

"I can give you a ride."

"Thanks but I don't want to waste my bus transfer."

Tanner Blue hugged Grace. "Nice sweater."

"My mother makes me wear this thing whenever my grandma visits. Grandma gave it to me. She knows I hate the colors but *she* loves them. That woman thinks she knows what's best for everybody."

Tanner Blue watched Grace rush past shelves of cereal and disappear to the left at the end of the aisle.

I taught that child how to read. Is that why her words carry so much weight with me? I didn't feel by myself until she left me alone wondering if her grandmother, 'that woman,' only thinks she knows what's best for everybody, of if she does know. What do I know?

Distracted, Tanner Blue wandered through the store. She picked up Nile's favorite whole-grain loaf. So she thought. Double-checking, she corrected herself. In the aisle of plastic plates and toothpicks, she found paper towels and examined roll after roll.

None of the designs measured up to the masterpiece she created one summer in her teens, so she finally settled on plain, recycled towels the color of a paper bag. Her towels rolled out like a long, paper quilt. Bold colors and patterns blanketed white space, raising concerns with the manufacturer about costs of extra ink. Up against a deadline and plagued by poor planning, they used Tanner Blue's concept, which caused a much needed spike in sales.

A red amaryllis near the check stand was the same color as the band that held Nile's braid in place. Who had taught him how to braid, or did he even practice that skill? What made him so friendly? Not once had Tanner Blue been the first to invite a man to spend any of his time with her, yet she did not expect to be noticed by men. When she was, she looked for love, always discovering how different searching was from finding.

Lines leading to the five cash registers were longer than Tanner Blue expected. The express lane stretched out the most, so she did not bother to count her items to see if they were below or above the cutoff of twelve. Joining check stand 3, she noticed a stack of Styrofoam cups in the cart used by the woman in front of her. She visualized a thin, tight spiral starting at the base of each cup, winding its way toward the rim. Adding colors to the spirals gave them a sense of motion borrowed from hummingbirds, lady bugs, and Saturn's rings.

The woman placed the whitened cups on the black conveyor belt along with bacon, eggs, soymilk, multivitamins, and vodka. Tanner Blue placed the gray-ribbed, rubber separator after the woman's items and began unloading her own cart.

The sandy-haired, male checker slowly scanned each of the woman's items and asked, "Did you find everything you were looking for?"

She snapped her fingers, which were the color of nonfat milk. "You still carry those date-nut cakes? You know the ones I mean."

"I *love* those things. We haven't gotten any in for a while. Have you tried the cherry ones?"

"I don't much care for cherries." The woman stroked her red fingernails.

"Really, they all taste the same." The checker laughed.

"I'll go get me one...." The woman glanced in a random direction.

"Stay put. I'll be right back."

Tanner pushed her cart out of the way of a white-man who got on line behind her and put another separator behind her groceries. He thanked her as the checker returned, a bit out of breath.

"There you go. Got you the last one."

"Why, bless your heart. What flavor?"

"Blueberry."

"That's better than cherry."

They both laughed.

"No problem."

The woman looked at the display above the cash register. She dug deep in the pockets of her jeans, pulled out a twenty, and received her change from the checker. A bagger asked if she needed help outside to her car.

"Oh, honey, I can manage. I hope I don't look like I need help with these few things."

"Not at all, miss. Bye now." The checker waved at her.

Tanner Blue took the woman's place in line and greeted the checker. Hastily, he weighed her apples and blurted out, "What kind are these?"

"Cortlands."

"How much a pound?"

"A dollar, I think."

He took a count-to-ten type breath. Flipped through a list and punched in a price. Methodically worked his way through the rest of her groceries.

"Twelve seventy-three." He held out his hand.

Tanner Blue placed exact change in his right palm. The checker took it and gave her a receipt. Started ringing up the next customer with a friendly, "Hello." A bagger packed Tanner Blue's groceries, put them in her cart, and moved on to the white-man behind her.

Outside, in the haze, Tanner Blue wondered how Grace made it through her own line. Placing her goods in the trunk, Tanner Blue thought of the whiteness of Styrofoam cups and how much she needed color.

~5~

Paris Art Supplies was more cluttered than Tanner Blue remembered until she realized it was largely due to a mural of the redwoods that took up all four walls. An outline of the Eiffel Tower peeked between distant tree trunks waiting to be filled in unless the artist had decided the picture was complete.

Was it?

Her teacher, Andre Moore, always said, 'You know you're done if adding or subtracting *anything* would ruin *everything*.' Andre was easy to pay attention to, a tree-tall black-man with skin the color of graham crackers but smooth like his voice and manner.

Studying the finer details of the mural — a nest of black birds in the upper-right corner, clouds reflecting specks of green from the trees, and the daystar, muted by a thin screen of blue-gray fog — Tanner Blue tried to determine for herself whether the mural felt finished. Indecisive, she wondered what Henry Tanner would say.

The question profiled her as she went up one aisle and down another, placing erasers, pencils, brushes, canvas boards, and gloss gel mixing medium in her aqua shopping cart. House-brand acrylics were on sale and she chose fuchsia, apricot, black and white. Crimson. Blues — cerulean, cornflower, and periwinkle. Blue-green. Out of habit, and not expecting to find it, she also looked for Tanner Blue.

She had been told and retold that it did not exist, so she found none there.

Thumbing through books about technique, she put them down before too long, not one to follow instructions. Looking at several sizes of sketchbooks, she refrained from buying one that was 20 inches square, haunted by the memory of its abandoned counterparts holed up in the shed.

There was no line at the cash register. According to fashion magazines Tanner Blue sometimes skimmed at the library, the female checker was *ethnic,* meaning, her long hair, hazel eyes, and light skin made you guess exactly why she could not pass for white.

"Can I help you find anything?" The checker recited that line pleasantly as if auditioning for a small part in a big play.

"I'm looking for the color, *Tanner Blue.*"

The checker looked through a tattered catalog and soon put it aside. Then she studied Tanner Blue for a moment that seemed like ages. "Maybe you have to mix it up yourself."

Tanner Blue looked at the shades of blue in her aqua cart. Tried to picture the blues she had seen in Henry Tanner's paintings. As she emptied her cart, she tried to imagine how to remember a color. Looking to the mural, she found no answer, but from her new perspective, the Eiffel Tower blended better with the redwoods than before.

"Who painted that mural?"

"My brother. I helped a little."

"How?"

"The Eiffel Tower and the ravens. I know he thinks I ruined it but he didn't say anything."

"Why ravens?"

"If you can get close enough to look them in the eye, they'll take you anywhere you want to go."

"You believe that?"

"I'll know when I get close enough."

"That explains it."

"What?"

"Why it might not be finished."

The checker smiled. "I told him it wasn't done."

Returning the smile, Tanner Blue asked, "How much do I owe you?"

"One-hundred dollars even, please."

Tanner Blue pulled a yellow wallet from her cloth, Guatemalan shoulder bag. She surrendered five wrinkled twenties and pocketed the receipt. To her, the cashier's parting "Thank you" translated to "Happy Birthday," which Tanner Blue accepted as a command.

Driving home, Tanner Blue missed the exit for Tourmaline Beach. The sky was a transparent blue and the daystar's rays had never felt as soothing. The Pacific surf seemed more at ease with itself, as if it had grown into the full power of its name. A raven perched on a dull, green freeway sign that read, "Mistral 1½," snatching Tanner Blue from a world she wanted to enter fully and explore. As sheer reflex, she turned off the freeway and made a hard left. Curved onto the winding road that lured her south past coastal pines overgrown with Spanish moss. A selfless sun with flames for fingertips pointed along that path. Pinkies poised, those warm hands lifted a blouse of light mist from tree tops, birds' nests, and lapping tongues of waves. Sea stacks held their postures against gangs of gusty wind. A full moon etched its face in broad daylight, ruling sky, stars, sea and souls.

Tanner Blue turned onto an unmarked road, opting for a shortcut home. She pulled into her driveway and parked in the space closest to the house. There was room for one more car to the right of hers, beside a thicket of junipers that swept north and south along the ridge. Ice plants with yellow and pink flowers tumbled downward, headed off by sand. Afternoon sun slapped the side of the house sharply with its heavy hand. It washed out the pale blue-green of the shingles that covered both the roof and siding, lightening it to gray. Spotlight sun and restless colors made her want to paint.

Like a bouquet, her new tools folded into her arms once sprung from the trunk of the car. Their weight equaled the blast of sunlight against the side of the house as she lugged them to the shed, opened the door, and set them down on the workbench. She placed a new canvas board on the easel, thankful it was not occupied by any of her sooner efforts, lurking.

The room was too crowded. Old canvases on the floor, the package and cards from the morning, newcomers heaped onto the workbench, adding up to clutter. There was little room left for air until she opened the window in front of the workbench. She let the faucet run out all the rust from the sink, wishing it was that easy to clear her mind. Filled a jar with water. Queuing up the new paints like pool balls, Tanner Blue wished she could shoot them into all the right pockets on the canvas. After gathering up the old paints, she started to throw them away, but instead left them in their own pile of memory. Wedged the old canvases behind them in a corner. She laid the new brushes across her old palette.

Tanner Blue was ready. Everything was in its proper place. She closed her eyes and tried to remember how to begin a painting. How had she done it before? No, how must she do it, now? Why couldn't she just jump right in? Most of all, what became of the energy that pushed her from the car, to the shed, and abandoned her so quickly?

"Tannerblue."

For a split second, the voice seemed to speak from inside her head until she recognized it more clearly. Slowly, she turned around.

"Nile."

"I hope I'm not intruding."

"I'm just thinking about...trying to clear my head." She massaged her temples.

"How about that walk?"

Tanner Blue looked from all the objects she was holding hostage in the shed, to Nile. She felt lightheaded, afraid that if she walked away right then, she might never even try to paint again. But maybe stepping away was in perfect order so she could return with feet more certain of her destination. Yes, that would be the better test—to see if anything could keep her from painting before the end of that same day.

~7~

Sun set and moon rose like mimes' hands measuring the weight of air. That music of the spheres stirred ocean, air—invisible stars and planets—into strings, flutes, and baby tambourines that sang one simple song of unity. Meteors interfered, rallying forces of asteroids, comets, and the occasional black hole that led to new beginnings. *Azul celeste*, sky blue, behaved like liquid. It poured into fog insistent as passion, determined as patience. Seabirds gathered, lazy ones attuned to leftovers, independents aware that they were predators and prey. Dogs and people drank every ounce of a true summer day that licked its way along the shore of Tourmaline Beach.

Gazing toward the hills packed tight with redwoods, Tanner Blue realized that she had done the unthinkable—she had indeed neglected the beach by taking easy access for granted. Life and art imitated each other as she saw Andre's series of seaside paintings reflected in the landscape. But neither Andre nor his paintings were at her side—Nile was and it was quiet enough for her to crave knowledge of his thoughts as they walked south beside the shore.

"Nile—you haven't said a word. What's on your mind?"

"Long week. Just trying to let it go."

"Tell me, so you can."

"I had this meeting with my graduate advisor about my thesis proposal—he's the chair of forestry. I can't tell if he doesn't understand what I'm trying to do or if he just isn't interested."

"What's the title?"

"'Reconnecting Urban Minority Populations with Natural Environments.' I've been working with different community-based organizations involved in sending kids to summer camp, running after-school programs, that sort of thing. I want to do national research, interviews, to find out the long-term impact of exposure to nature on people of color who come from inner cities."

"What exactly did your advisor say?"

"I don't know."

"What do you mean?"

"I mean, I was listening, but he talked so fast that by the time he finished, I felt like he was trying to make me feel stupid."

"You didn't, did you?"

"No. I asked him to restate what he said because it wasn't making sense."

"Did he?"

"He said if I couldn't follow him, maybe I was in the wrong major."

"What did you say?"

"I *wanted* to tell him maybe he's in the wrong profession if he can't handle a simple request. I *wanted* to say, 'Fuck that, man— would you just do your job?' I asked if he was going to approve my thesis. He said he wasn't convinced that my project was *meaningful*.

What kind of shit is that? We went back and forth to the point he said he'd reconsider."

"Do you think he's testing you?"

"Oh, he's definitely doing that."

"Maybe you intimidate him for all kinds of reasons."

"Even though he's got the power?"

"Not all of it."

"I always try to ask myself if I'm seeing what's really there."

"Do any of the other grad students have that problem?"

"I've asked a few and they looked at me like I was trying to start something, except for this one Hupa brother from the reservation. He didn't come right out and agree but he did invite me to a sweat lodge cleansing ceremony." He shrugged. "Got no idea what to expect."

Tanner Blue slowed down, measuring one footstep carefully in front of the next.

"Nile?"

"Hmm?"

"Will you be the first black-man to get a graduate degree in forestry?"

"I can't think about that right now. I'm focused on getting that degree in my hands."

"That's what matters, Nile. It can be the strangest instinct though, knowing you're being treated differently and why. I'm proud you're studying forestry."

He smiled. "When I was a kid, my favorite thing to do was climb trees, mainly in the Berkeley hills. I feel like I understand them—we understand each other and I want to help other people have that experience." Nile stood still. "Tannerblue—I'm sorry!"

"Why the apology?" Stopping, she looked directly at Nile, startled by the sudden absence of his voice.

"This is no way to celebrate your birthday. Listen, I couldn't help but notice all the art stuff back there in the shed. I didn't know you were an artist."

Tanner Blue took off her sandals, placing one in each hand before testing the water. It was cold enough to make the sand feel warm beneath her soles once she continued walking with Nile at her side. Thin clouds traveled over the tops of hillside redwoods, confirming that art imitated life because motion could not be trapped on any canvas. Poetry had no legs, tongue, or throat. Notes on sheets of music made no sound. But art and life needed one another, simply because each existed by the grace of light and shadow.

"Henry Tanner, he's an artist. Andre Moore, he's an artist."

"I don't know anything about them but I'm trying my best to know Tannerblue."

In his eyes, she detected his interest in her. Tanner Blue shuddered at that thought, and from a slight chill that pushed forth from the flowing tide. Already, the fear of losing his attention threatened taking any risks.

"Mind if we walk a little faster? It's getting cold."

"Sure." Nile untied the sweater whose arms were looped around his neck and hung it loosely over Tanner Blue's shoulders. She nodded, 'thank you,' as she put her sandals back on. Re-warmed feet made it easier for her to talk.

"I took some art classes off and on for a few years. Painting. Drawing."

"At the college?"

"Yeah, from Andre Moore. You can't miss him."

Nile stopped. "Wait a minute—tall brother?" He raised a hand above his head.

Tanner Blue nodded.

"We do the 'nod,' you know, exchange a few words, but he always seems like he's in another world."

"That's him, even when you get to know him. We did still lives."

"Bowls of fruit?"

She laughed. "Any objects that seemed interesting. He kept jazz playing in the background. Mostly, he talked to each student and tried to help us express what we wanted to come out on the canvas."

"You stay in touch?"

She shook her head. "We run into each other on campus every now and then, usually at the library."

"Why'd you stop taking classes?"

"He invited me to one of his shows, down in San Francisco. I went."

"So, what happened at the show?"

"It was at this big, fancy gallery South of Market. I underdressed and felt all out of place, but the space was packed and I got there late, so I didn't stand out. I'd only seen his paintings before at small shows up here.

"The gallery was like ones I've seen pictures of in SoHo. Papi was going to take me to SoHo when we went to New York but we didn't get to it. I invited him to Andre's show but he said he just wasn't up to it. I was disappointed. Angry, really. I thought he'd be happy to see another creative black-man being successful. He wouldn't even cross the bridge from Oakland. Didn't even apologize."

"Did you speak up about it?"

She shook her head.

"You were telling me about the gallery."

"It had the highest ceilings, lots of open, clean space. Live jazz quartet from Chicago with a vocalese artist."

"*Vocalese*? I love jazz."

"Yeah. They sing and write lyrics for instrumentals."

Nile nodded. "Go on."

"The people and their clothes were so elegant. Long tables of food and wine. Even though I grew up in Oakland and had been to San Francisco plenty of times, I felt like it was my first time in a big city. Then I started looking at Andre's paintings.

"The pieces at the show were abstract. There was a series of canvases from tiny to quite large and each successive one had one subtle detail added. In a sense, they were like puzzles, mostly pastel colors. That work was completely different from the landscapes I was used to—they were so true to life, you felt like you were a part of the scene. In the city, he was different, I was different, his paintings, everything felt new.

"There was this long line of people waiting to see him. The closer I got, the more they crowded me. I must have stopped moving forward. This sister standing next to him. She was beautiful. I never knew anything about his personal life."

"Did you want to be in her place?"

Tanner Blue shook her head and stuffed her hands in her pockets. "I didn't but the funny thing is, that's the closest I've felt to success. People were writing checks and the woman was collecting them. That's when those endless white walls started closing in. I had to get out of that place."

"You did get to talk to him, right?"

She shook her head. "I couldn't. I drove back up here that same night."

"I don't get it, Tannerblue."

"It was the money, Nile. The prices. All those checks. Something someone said to me."

Nile opened his mouth. Tanner Blue placed her fingers on his lips. "Doesn't matter who it was, Nile. Does it?"

Gently, he removed her fingers and kissed them. "No, it doesn't." He put his arm around her and lowered his voice.

"What happened when you got back?"

"I dropped out of his class and neither of us has ever said a word about that show."

"But you kept painting after that, right?"

"Wrong."

"Tell me something, Tannerblue. Forget about what anybody said, no matter who it was. Did you ever even *want* to make money off your work?"

Tanner Blue's throat tightened. "This has been the longest day!" She wiped away welled-up tears that were at home in the vast shadow of twilight.

"There's more to it, Tannerblue. You'll see."

Nile's arm across her shoulders lifted years of weight from Tanner Blue's soul. That load swept upward like a balloon, its loose string happily released from the grip of some sweaty hand. Drawing heavily on air, she took a first breath for a second time. Returning it to the atmosphere, she slid her hand across Nile's lower back and let it settle on the right side of his waist.

Turquoise skies stained an outline of the moon amid a destiny of stars. Surf trickled past the sandaled feet of the woman, the thick heels of the man, ebbing only when it safely saw them home.

~8~

Light blue, cloth napkins were folded unevenly beside dark blue ceramic plates. Wild salmon topped with capers and spicy, steamed vegetables decorated each dish. A wooden bowl of salad sat in the middle of the round table beside a square, green vase of pink tulips. A bottle of merlot breathed deeply through its thin meniscus, whining orders that the flowers neglected to obey. The Tiffany lamp hung a bit off center above the table, reluctantly illuminating an oversized hummingbird feeding on a crooked olive branch.

Elbows firmly on the table, Tanner Blue folded her hands beneath her chin. "Nile, thank you—for your thoughtfulness, your time."

"Surprised?"

"Yes, and no."

They laughed and he poured their wine.

"Listen, I'm not much good with toasts but I got you a little something." He reached into a cabinet above the kitchen sink. Returned to the table and handed her a small, blue box tied with a thin, red ribbon.

Her fingers traced the teardrop shape of the bow.

"Does it make sense to say, 'I'm speechless'?"

"No."

They laughed again.

"I know better than to ask if I can wait to open it."

"Good!"

Tanner Blue carefully undid the ribbon and removed the top of the box. She smoothed out the piece of purple tissue paper that stood between her and the gift.

"Such brilliant colors. What's your favorite color, Nile?"

"I'm looking right at it."

She looked right at him, plagued by memories of men she had shared everything with except love that hung around for good.

"Nile, whatever it is, it's too much. I mean, I don't even know when your birthday is."

"Middle of October."

"How old?"

"I'll be twenty-eight. Do me a favor?"

"Tell me."

"Don't tell me I seem mature, especially for my age."

She smiled. "So, I wouldn't be the first woman to say that."

He smiled back and nodded toward the undressed box Tanner Blue held in her hands. "Would you give that to me so I can finish the job?"

"Okay, okay. Let me see what this is."

Slowly, she drew a deep breath. Peeled back the tissue paper, handling it as delicately as a birth certificate. In the center of the box, a blue rock rested in the cradle of its own comfort. It was dark and clear with many facets. She held it up to the Tiffany lamp.

"Nile, how beautiful! Every shade of blue I've ever seen is in this stone."

"It's an Aqua Aura crystal. They put it through a chemical process using gold."

Tanner Blue pressed the crystal to her palm and felt its pulse. A slight vibration spread from the crystal to her hand and radiated through her body. She looked at Nile and said, "It feels alive."

"I got it from this Native-Indian shop up in Mistral. The woman who sold it to me said it's good for anything you want help with. All you have to do is ask." Nile pointed his chin toward her plate and picked up his fork. "I don't know about you but I can talk and eat at the same time."

Tanner Blue took a bite of her salmon.

"You think it's magic?"

He glanced sideways at her and said, "Let me know."

When they finished eating, Nile cleared the table and to-gether, they cleaned up the kitchen. Tanner Blue took her crystal, the merlot, and both of their glasses to the living room. She placed them on the coffee table in front of the maroon sofa and poured the glasses full. As usual, she repositioned the moss-green throw pillows on the sofa until she was comfortable. Used her toes to unfold a bent edge of the olefin carpet beneath the table. The rug was patterned with mul-ticolored squares and pyramid shapes on a background of dappled blue and yellow. Often, Tanner Blue tried to imagine the process of gathering raw materials for the carpet, designing the patterns and, finally, weaving it all into an artist's completed vision. Two chairs that matched the sofa occupied the other side of the rug. One held a large, persimmon colored comforter. The other was paired with a red-orange ottoman.

Tanner Blue had painted the walls by herself. Maize. Three years ago, once she bought the house. Her father inspected it, assuring her it was in very good condition at twenty years old. For the first time, she saw him in a rush. He could barely make it through the day and insisted on driving back to Oakland first thing the following morning. He promised to come back when she moved in and help her paint. She was too preoccupied to talk about his uneasiness then. Looking at the paint, it seemed faded before its time, like a dream confused with sleep.

Tanner Blue started a fire in the pellet stove and let it be the only source of light. The stove was Perla's idea. Perla had grown into extended family since the day she met Tanner Blue at the bus station and helped her settle into the dorm. Perla's cousin sold the stoves and gave Tanner Blue a discount. Nile was enthusiastic about their efficiency and environmental friendliness when he interviewed to become Tanner Blue's roommate.

Dual-paned sliding glass doors led to the deck that spanned the west side of the house, keeping surplus cold and dampness at bay. The maple, hardwood floors looked warm, coaxing frigid air toward heat.

Tanner Blue rubbed her feet on the rug to erase a slight chill. She bent over and massaged her toes.

"I can do that." Nile started to kneel. Tanner Blue touched his leg to stop him, before he got too close. He straightened up.

"You've done more than enough, Nile. Dinner, the crystal, the walk." She folded her legs beneath her. Reached forward and passed him a glass of wine. He winked at her.

"So, what was in that package?"

"What package?"

"The one that came this morning."

"I forgot! I should go open it...." She unfolded her legs and stood, her eyes level with his shoulders.

"Wait. Please." He placed his hand on the side of her neck. Stroked her jaw with his thumb. "I have to tell you something."

"Nile, why are you...?"

"That's what I have to tell you. It's in your eyes."

"What is?"

"The answer to your question."

"But I haven't even...."

"The day I came here to check out your extra room, truth be told, it was a struggle to keep my mind on finding a new place to live. Your eyes, they see things, they take you places, Tannerblue. All I could think was how I'd like to go there with you."

He kissed her.

"Nile, I hate to make mistakes...."

He rested his hands lightly on her shoulders. "What's the biggest mistake you've ever made?"

"I can't think of it right now. I can't think."

"You know what, Tannerblue? I only believe in experiences."

"They can be good or bad, Nile. I only want what's good."

Nile took one step away from her.

"Do *exactly* what you want right now."

He smelled like ocean and the breath of eucalyptus. She inhaled, towed into the ample beauty of the day turned night.

"Thanks for letting me borrow your sweater." She undid the sleeves from around her shoulders and let the sweater fall to the carpet. Placed her hands on his chest and slid them to his upper back. When she tilted up her head and kissed him, his mouth tasted like *Sangría*.

"Mmmm." He licked her lips.

"Mmmmm....."

Their full embrace was an anchor — weightless, solid, pure. Kiss after kiss dug a tunnel, soul to soul, body to mind. Though they sank down to the carpet, they were lifted up to their place in its universe. It was there that two pair of hands swiftly undressed both bodies, leaving only skin. Skin and hair. Lips, tongues, muscles. Thighs and toes. Random motion transformed to rhythm, relentless as a wave.

Lying on her side, facing Nile, Tanner Blue realized she had only looked at him before. Seeing him meant feeling him, touching him all over, watching the stable smile in his eyes each time he came close to entering her for the first time. The first time. It felt like the first time though she would not bleed or hurt like then. It was the first time it had felt like the first time since then. How many men? Should she make a birthday-candle wish for five to be her lucky number?

Nile pulled Tanner Blue close to him, pressed against her, wrapped her leg over his thigh, across his back. Pressed, kissed, looked deep into her eyes.

"Tannerblue?"

"Mmmm...." She gripped his shoulders.

"You are a dream come true."

He inched into her slowly, as he would if it were her first time. Maneuvered her onto her back and moved with her, gratified that it was not her first time. The tighter she gripped, the more he held back until she exhausted every last seed of his energy. For one endless moment, they shared a rippling pulse. Their full embrace was an anchor—weightless, softened, pure.

Nile kissed Tanner Blue's forehead. Broke away long enough to get the comforter and all the throw pillows to make their bed right on the floor.

She rested her head on his chest. "Did you plan this?"

"No way I could have but I tell you what—the real thing was better than any fantasy."

"I can't see myself that way."

"You're not supposed to." He smoothed her hair away from her face.

"Nile, tell me what's wrong with you." She spoke to the center of his chest.

"Huh?" He turned her toward him.

"You can't be perfect, can you?"

"Sure, why not?"

She laughed. "Really. Tell me all your faults."

"They're like mistakes for you—I can't think of any right now."

"Maybe one?" She lifted her index finger.

"What would that be?"

"You seemed slightly jealous when I was telling you about Andre."

"I just wanted to make sure you weren't involved with anyone."

"Now you're certain?"

He propped himself up on one elbow. "Are you seeing someone else?" All traces of smiles were gone.

"You first."

"I don't play games, Tannerblue."

"Neither do I." She stood up and got dressed.

"What's going on?"

"I want to open my present and read my cards before midnight." She went in her room and checked her clock. It was 10:47. When she turned around, Nile was standing there, wrapped in the comforter.

"I don't want to ruin things, birthday girl." He walked toward her. "I'm glad we got our first fight out of the way so fast. Can we kiss and make up?"

"That would be a mistake."

He stood still. "Only if your mind is made up."

"I tried to warn you...."

"And I tried to make your birthday happy."

"You have, Nile. You have. Right now, I need some fresh air and some space."

"Just give me one more kiss so we won't stay angry."

She did not completely want to say what came out: "If we're really angry, a kiss won't change a thing."

"When you come back, can we spend the rest of this night together? I hate to sleep alone."

"You're telling me you don't *have* to sleep alone. I *know* that."

"That's not what I meant at all. You've never seen me with anyone, have you, Tannerblue?"

"I've never *seen* you…."

"Now, who's jealous?"

"That's not jealousy. That has to do with trust."

"You don't trust me?"

"I don't *know* you!"

Tanner Blue stormed out of her room, rolling thunder through the house and out the sliding glass doors. She got as far as the deck.

"Shit!"

I should bring that damn crystal.

She turned around and Nile was holding it up. Rushing back inside their house, she took the crystal from him and pressed her lips into his cheek.

One of the tubes in the fluorescent light above the workbench flick-
ered, keeping rhythm with a slight buzzing sound. Tanner Blue felt
like she was in a black-and-white photo, until she placed the Aqua
Aura crystal on the windowsill. Immediately, it trapped a shaft of
moonlight, striping the crystal from top to bottom and causing it to
glow. That extra light turned itself on Tanner Blue in such a way that
she observed herself as she imagined someone else would see her. At
first, she thought her dull reflection in the latticed window was responsible for that sensation. Then, she actually felt herself being pho-
tographed in black and white, back when she was a child. Or, was
she the one taking the picture?

The sudden cold consorted with a fluttering noise that came
from outside the shed, both forces making Tanner Blue shudder. She
listened for the sound to repeat, relieved that it was replaced by
crashing waves and whistling wind.

The shed was roughly the same size as the room she grew up
in. Through high school, she stayed up late listening to jazz on the
radio in that room doing homework and making pencil drawings
from picture books of lions, barns, and horses etched in ink. Then
came pastel sunsets and abstract sketches with technical pens. Expecting an answer from the shed, she tried hard to remember when

she had first used a pen or pencil for something other than a school assignment.

She paced, trying to remember, acutely aware that she was watching herself again, right there in black and white. This absence of true color felt so unnatural, reducing everything to shadows. But there was something familiar about it. Glancing at all the little squares in the latticed window, an image of the color TV in the corner of her room sharpened in her mind. The reception was bad except for the channel that ran a drawing program, two nights each week at 11:30. No matter how she adjusted the antenna, that channel came in as black and white.

The artist was a black-woman named Jiaré who wore elaborate head wraps and flowing garments. Initially, Tanner Blue was frustrated not to see the clothes in color until she got into the groove of filling in those details with her imagination. Then, she looked forward to that exercise.

Tanner Blue was in the shed because she needed some sustaining thing to look forward to. Sitting on the bar stool at the workbench, she weighed the package and each card in her hands. Decided to open her father's blue envelope first, simply because it felt the lightest.

A brown, cloth doll with black pigtails stared back at her from the front of a greeting card. Her red lips were frozen into a stiff smile that matched the tension keeping her angled eyes half open. She seemed so weary that Tanner Blue wanted to offer her someplace to rest her feet, which twisted outward, no doubt placing undue stress on the poor thing's knees. Or, perhaps she could use a hot cup of tea—the white background of the card might be quite cold. No longer able to endure this child's discomfort, Tanner Blue flipped open the card, catching the check for $100 before it fell to the workbench. A black-and-white photograph was taped inside the left half of the card. The picture showed Tanner Blue crunched between both parents, leaning toward her father. They were all sitting on some grass, smiling. Water filled the background. Green rolling hills. The sun proved itself the brightest star.

Her father took pictures in spurts and she had memorized all of them along with their stories, except for the photo staring at her. Not only was she certain to be seeing it for the first time, she had no recollection of the day. Who had taken it? She was wearing a denim short set with a sailboat in the middle of the top and anchors on each of the pockets of the bottom. Her father wore a light-blue, short-sleeved shirt and khaki pants, his hair parted on the left side and neatly combed. Her mother had on a long, straight, lavender dress with large, white buttons down the front. She looked pretty.

Tanner Blue loved her father's handwriting, hard as it was to decode. She read what he had written in her card:

Dear Blue,

Stone gave me this picture a long time ago. He took it when we visited that place I helped him build up in Clear Lake. I wanted to save it for a special occasion to help you remember a good time. Buy yourself something nice with the money. You deserve nice things. Happy birthday! So glad you were born.

Love,

Papi

P.S. The baby doll made me think of the first time I held you.

Often, her father said he knew the depth of love the first time he held her. The card, the words, and the picture made her know that she was loved in a way that let her love. Growing up, Tanner Blue was happiest when she had her father all to herself, which was rare because he was always working. He would take her with him on weekends or during the summer when he was finishing up jobs, when it was safe to have his child on site.

Studying the picture, she tried to remember one happy time alone with her mother. An undercurrent got in the way, the one that eventually led to an argument between her parents. Tanner Blue had interfered, taking her father's side.

Closing the card, Tanner Blue shut her eyes and clapped her hands over her ears but an opportunistic voice forced itself on her.

"If you're going to meddle, child, then be fair! You remember this — it takes two to argue and your precious father, he is not a saint."

Eyes open, Tanner Blue tried to make sense of her spat with Nile. Who had pushed the button? She would rather be hurt than cause the hurting. He wanted to make up and she wanted to know what would make that necessary.

She stared at her mother's aerogramme a long time before picking it up. It lay heavily in her hand as she opened it, finding a letter and something else wrapped in a blank sheet from an airmail tablet.

Child,

Where you were born keeps its hold on you. I have always known this. I send you this picture so you know that I was once a child.

You have always thought you were a woman. Now that you are one, you could come see me sometime.

Your mother

For a moment, Tanner Blue tried to believe that her parents got together and decided to surprise her with those pictures—that they actually had a long-distance discussion, reminiscing about a past redeemed through healing powers of time. Somehow, that imagination helped her see the three of them as any other family with differences strengthened by reddened bonds of blood.

Slowly, she unfolded the paper blanketing the photograph her mother sent. A skinny girl sat on the top step leading to a porch, elbow propped on her knee, chin resting in her hand. Her head was tilted to one side as if she listened carefully for her future. She squinted and smiled at the same time, daring the photographer to test skills beyond their limits to that point. Self-aware, the child's persona demanded a historical honesty that testified to youth.

Tanner Blue turned over the picture and read the jagged script along its bottom border:

Marguerite at 9

Returning it face up, she placed it beside the picture from her father. Comparing the two little girls, she looked for the slightest detail that would cause anyone to know they were related. One candidate was their braided hair—hers, two short, simple plaits falling away from a part down the center of her head. Tanner Blue counted at least four braids in the front of her mother's head, one of them tied neatly with a ribbon. They were both around the same age. What was on her mother's mind then, and as she slid the photograph into the aerogramme? Tanner Blue had never seen her mother as hopeful. What else had she, herself, not seen?

The fluttering sound returned, above the shed, and then there was a thud that caused Tanner Blue's heart to skip a beat before accelerating. She breathed deeply to slow down the pounding in her chest, convincing herself that the outer sound was natural, that she was the one who was out of place after having abandoned the shed for so long. Outside, moonlight streaked the flowing tide. That silver path welcomed her toward existence lacking affinity with time. But how? How could she accept that invitation?

Absentmindedly, she undid the brown paper wrapping on Kalina's gift. Untaped the sides of the brown corrugated box and folded back its upper flaps. Smiled at the face of her best friend's birthday card, which bore a stick drawing of two figures holding hands. She read the words, inside:

> *Dear Tan,*
>
> > *Guess who?*
>
> *Your sister, love,*
>
> > *Kali*

Tanner Blue smiled, glad Kalina continued to resist sending cards that said, 'Happy Birthday,' tacked on to someone else's words.

She set the card upright on the workbench and peeled back the brown tissue paper in the box. Squares of cloth stared back at her. The entire length of the fabric was roughly fifteen inches and when Tanner Blue lifted it out of the box, she discovered that the fabric was folded in half. Smoothing the entire piece on the workbench revealed ten squares altogether. She looked through the box for an explanation but the squares seemed determined to speak for themselves. Turning them over, she found words scribbled on the back of each one. They were hard to read but finally, she deciphered what they said:

Monkey Wrench

Wagon Wheel

Bear's Paw

Crossroads

Log Cabin

Shoofly

Bow Ties

Flying Geese

Drunkard's Path

Stars[1]

She tried to match each description to its cloth pattern, flipping the fabric back and forth. It appeared to be a simple, colorful jumble of shapes. Observing more closely, she noticed that each piece was remarkably unique. Colors between squares did not repeat themselves and no color dominated. Touching the cloth, the texture reminded her of a softened version of dried acrylic paint.

Tanner Blue's heart skipped another beat as she remembered the awkward conversation with Kalina that started her birthday. She accused Kalina of not knowing her but was it possible that her best friend did know a personal thing or two that Tanner Blue, herself, could not see? Had that been the case as far back as fourth grade?

Despite the confusion inside her head, everything had its place in front of Tanner Blue—paints, palette, brushes. A brand new canvas board waited on the easel, but what about the old ones? Should she pick up where she left off or pretend they did not exist? Tanner Blue wanted to forget about them until she realized she did not know exactly what she would be ignoring. She wanted to mix paint but the tubes became a stubborn foreign language and the palette was a wasteland. She could not stain a clean and innocent canvas without the former knowledge.

Tanner Blue walked over to the corner. She wanted to apologize to the canvases for neglecting them as if she were a spoiled child busy attracting her next object of desire. She built all four of the canvases, applied the gesso and staples. Made them all the same size, 36×24-inches, for simplicity. How could she express this remorse to abandoned works of art? She started by turning them over, one at a time, until all four were facing her, backs against the wall. Gradually, their rage gave way to understanding and forgiveness.

Tanner Blue remembered painting the smooth, terra cotta, African drum with the hemp twists securing the skin top surface to its base. She touched the canvas, feeling three dimensions. That painting was her very first effort since designing the paper towels in high school. Contacting it resumed a conversation that was oblivious to any interruption. The challenges had been creating a soft shadow and being conscious of light sources as organic parts of compositions. Tanner Blue had given those colors, that canvas, and the drum her best efforts and she liked what she saw.

The second painting was of a large rhododendron plant. It was a study in *negative space* — the air surrounding everything that appeared solid. The thrill of understanding that concept returned with a newness like making love with Nile for the first time. She could not help but smile.

Then there was the obligatory bowl of fruit with vegetables added for character—Mexican mango, Japanese eggplant, pluot plum, Gala apple, Valencia orange, and Italian zucchini. Tanner Blue made the bowl from red clay in a ceramics class her first term at the college. She let it dry thoroughly, etched a row of circles with dots in their centers along the side, then burnished the bowl with a smooth stone over a period of days. Sometime later, Tanner Blue discovered that the circle-dot design was a symbol of wholeness and completion in parts of North Africa.

She clearly remembered Andre's instruction for the fourth piece. He said, "Paint something abstract. You think that's easy, right? Always, remember to be intentional." Sitting for the longest time in front of the blank canvas, it had seemed to get bigger and grow emptier the longer Tanner Blue faced it. The assignment forced her to think about what it meant to start a painting. Her choices were to wait for a picture to create itself in her mind and then try to reproduce that image. She could sharpen her awareness of sights colored by sensations and be ready to seize the ones that inspired. Or, she could just start mixing paint and filling up the canvas, letting herself be guided by the rhythm of colors and brush strokes. A combination had potential—she could develop some general idea about what she wanted to paint, start it, and trust that if she could begin she could finish. That had been her thinking. That had been how she attempted to paint the color, *Tanner Blue.*

Looking more closely at each painting, they struck her as being finished yet incomplete.

What made me stop one and go on to the next?

Tanner Blue dragged her stool over to the easel and installed herself firmly into the seat, which was uncomfortable and accepting. When she was face to face with the blank canvas, the fluttering sound announced itself at the outer ledge of the windowsill. The outline of a raven, larger than life, was framed by four latticed window panes. The bird faced south and raised its left wing, the one closest to where Tanner Blue sat. The raven's head tilted toward her and its smooth, curved beak pointed at the canvas. For a split second, the Aqua Aura crystal on the windowsill, blacked out by the raven, seemed aligned with where Tanner Blue imagined the bird's heart to be. The raven tapped the bottom of the glass with its left foot, pointing to Tanner Blue's new paint brushes, which were spread across her palette like five fingers.

Pick one up.

Tanner Blue leaned closer to the raven. Looked it in the eye.

What happens if I don't?

The raven flapped one wing.

Absolutely nothing.

Tanner Blue walked over to the window. Pressed her right hand to the glass, expecting the raven to fly off. It flapped its other wing.

And if I do?

Cocking its head to one side, the raven lifted both wings.

We'll see.

A cry rose from the raven's throat, growing louder as it sang out to the fully risen moon. Tanner Blue rode that wave of sound, dizzy as she chose the largest brush with the thickest handle and coarsest bristles. Tightening her grip around that tool, she blended all of her blues on the stained, white palette. She applied the color of her name to the canvas and knew she was connected.

PART
Two

~10~

The sky speaks loudly in swirls of green, violet, and pink. It is danced upon by sapphire stars, and underpainted by a bluish black. Tanner Blue sits at the top of a meadow thick with wildflowers and tall grass, knees tucked to her chest, gently rocking back and forth. The meadow slopes down to a stream. Ribbons of rainbow moonlight ride upon the water's back, flowing in the four directions, brightening the sky. Shadowy outlines of human figures swim back and forth. Tanner Blue tries to count them but their numbers grow too quickly. One reaches out a hand to another, who brings someone else along.

Are you escaping or arriving?

They all stop suddenly and nod at her.

Yes? Both?

A man at the edge of the other bank shakes his head and kneels. Places something on the ground before disappearing with all the others. Tanner Blue runs down to the stream, hoping she can see what the man has left behind. It is too dark. The water, shallow or deep, separates her from full discovery. She never learned to swim.

"What brings you here?"

"My first memory, first thought. My first feeling."

"What were they?"

"I had no words when I was born."

"Exactly."

Her answer is an impulse.

"Who *exactly* are you?"

"*Blackton.*"

"Where are we?"

"*Nice of you to include me. You're in Blackton.*"

"I'm *in* you?"

"*Well, I was in you first. I'm your idea, Tanner Blue.*"

"How do you know my name?"

"*What did I just tell you?*"

"You're my idea. Of course I know my own name."

"*Very good. You have words now. So tell me — why are you here?*"

"To connect every point of my life, from the beginning to now."

"*Close your eyes.*"

"Why?"

"*Efficiency. What you'll experience will be the shortest distances between all those points. Trust me.*"

"But what am I trusting?"

"*The power of your imagination. It can show you anything you want to see, and before you ask I'll tell you — anything you can see is real.*"

"But, Blackton, I'm afraid of what I'll see."

"*More afraid of that than what you do not see?*"

"You mean, fear of the unknown?"

"*There's no such thing as the 'unknown,' Tanner Blue. What do you think believing is?*"

Tanner Blue sits at the bank of the stream. Across the meadow, a warm wind flows, which she interprets as Blackton smiling. Breath by breath, she relaxes and slowly closes her eyes. Bells and wind chimes sound, painting with the color blue. Her inner vision detects the cautious movement of the man across the water. His large eyes and smooth skin are the color of a coffee bean — his face, a mask that fills up all the space in Tanner Blue's mind. The serious expression he wears matches the words he speaks, which Tanner Blue cannot understand, so she is shocked to know what he is saying. He knows and tells the story of her life, much of it translates through sweeping gestures, high and low. Besides his face, his right hand is all she can see clearly. He holds up what appears to be a small, rusted piece of metal and says a word she has heard but cannot repeat before it escapes her entirely. She opens her eyes suddenly, ready to see new meanings. Instead, someone speaks.

Bare feet, a medium brown, are planted on the grass beside her. A yellow hem brushes their ankles, sweeping upward into a long-sleeved, snugly fitting dress that covers the body of the woman who has joined Tanner Blue in the meadow. Small, blue, crystal earrings sway beneath coils of thick, dark-brown hair swept back from her oval face.

Slowly, Tanner Blue stands and studies her. "Pardon me?"

"I said, tell me everything you know."

"That's impossible."

"It's the only way you'll get what you want."

"Wait a minute." Tanner Blue places a hand on the woman's shoulder. Touches her left cheek, feeling warm, solid flesh and bone. The woman looks into her eyes.

"I know you — Jiaré?"

"I'm glad you remember."

"But how could *you* know *me*? I watched you on...."

"Don't say that word here. It might surprise you to know that you're the only one who ever saw me."

"It might."

"Did you ever talk with anyone else about the program?"

"I must have told my best friend." Tanner Blue is startled that she does not want to mention that friend's name. She does not want to mention anything specific about her life before this moment with the one great exception that is the reason for her being here.

Jiaré turns suddenly and begins walking up the meadow. Her pace is steady and Tanner Blue follows quickly.

"They thought I'd be the best one to help you."

"*They?*"

"The Almáte."

"*Almáte?*"

"The others here in Blackton."

"*Almáte* — what does it mean?"

"It's the gesture used in greeting. I must ask you to do something, Tanner Blue."

"And that is?"

"Try to do more thinking and observing than asking. The answers will be more valuable."

At the top of the meadow, the sky filters into an even tone of lightening blue, camouflaging dimming stars. Distant, rolling hills and a broad, blue-green valley reveal no evidence of *others*, making it difficult for Tanner Blue to imagine where they might be, what they might be doing here.

"Where are we going?" It is so quiet that Tanner Blue expects to hear her voice echo. The only sound is the one made by her feet and Jiaré's as they pat along a smooth path sloping downward toward the valley.

"I'm taking you to your place."

"My place?"

"Yes, you asked for this."

"I know." Tanner Blue does not know nor does she want to appear ignorant. She resists asking the obvious question, *What am I getting myself into?*, certain its answer will be revealed.

Ahead, brown shadows take form as people who welcome her with nods and hands placed on their chests. Tanner Blue places her hand on her chest and nods back. The people do not stop or speak. They just keep moving forward, leisurely yet determined.

As the path winds closer to the valley, Tanner Blue and Jiaré pass several sandstone buildings painted mauve, yellow, and green. The road expands and contracts, giving Tanner Blue the sensation of being created in someone else's painting, which is when she realizes that she still holds a paintbrush in her hand. Waving it in the air, she becomes aware of all the colors that surround her—orange, pink, and yellow wildflowers at her feet and in the distance. Purple bushes, jade reeds. Tanner-Blue trees.

"We have a way to go, Tanner Blue. Go ahead, tell me."

As they walk, Tanner Blue soon realizes that she is counting each step she takes.

"Two hands, ten fingers, teaching me to count. My father taught me. One Friday night, he brought home this blackboard with the alphabet written around the borders in white script. Uppercase and lowercase with numbers underneath. He sat with me and went through all twenty-six letters. Taught me how to count up to 100. I was way ahead of all the other kids in kindergarten. Starting then, I knew love."

"Keep going." Jiaré brushes her fingertips along the tops of bushes as they walk. Each small, green leaf seems to grin beneath the comfort of her touch.

"I know how it feels to be away from home. Always. Isn't that funny?" Tanner Blue tries to laugh, but the sound that comes out knows nothing of humor. She wants Jiaré to say something and prove that she is listening and cares. Caring too much has been her own greatest enemy to making friends.

As if feelings can be measured.

Jiaré's voice travels into the valley, stretched out, open ended. "What else?"

"I know how to paint. That's how I ended up here." She holds up the paintbrush. "The first time I ever picked up one of these was in fourth grade when an art teacher tried to show me how to mix up flesh tone."

"Uh oh." Jiaré laughs. Tanner Blue does too, relieved to see a lighter dimension of her guide.

"She used lots of white with little flecks of brown, red, and yellow mixed in. I put a spot of it on the back of my hand and showed it to her. That was the first time I ever made a statement. Since then, it's been easier to express myself."

Jiaré walks up a short incline and stops on the doorstep of a small blue house overlooking the stream. "This is your place."

Tanner Blue looks around, seeking something solid to hold on to. She does not trust the dependability of a yellow railing on 'her' porch.

"You know, it's beautiful here. Thank you for the tour Jiaré, but I should probably be getting back." She looks to the path that has led her where she stands.

Jiaré places a hand on Tanner Blue's arm. "You must finish what you've started before you can go anywhere else. You know that."

"What do you mean?"

"The painting."

"Am I a *prisoner*?"

"*Prisoner*? Why wouldn't you want to stay here? You can do anything you want. You'll have everything you need. We're completely free."

"I want to be *free* to go back when I'm ready. I'm ready."

"Then, go ahead. No one here will stop you."

"How? I don't even know exactly how I got here. I was just sitting there...." She looks at the paintbrush. "I was just sitting there and then I picked up this brush. Maybe if I just put it back down." She places it on the ground and nothing happens.

"Looks like you have some things to figure out." Jiaré turns back toward the main path. Tanner Blue follows.

"Wait. What about a key?"

Jiaré laughs. "Just open the door." She speeds her pace and Tanner Blue keeps up.

"Where are you going?"

"*My* place."

"But, what am I supposed to do?"

"Everything you've ever dreamed of."

"But, I haven't told you everything I know."

"Show me through your painting. Perhaps you'll start to notice some connections." Jiaré begins to jog.

"Wait! Don't leave me, Jiaré! At least tell me, where is your place?"

"Ask anyone."

Tanner Blue looks around. "Who?!?"

Jiaré runs off, too fast for Tanner Blue to keep up. Stopping, out of breath, Tanner Blue tries to steady the flow of air in and out of her lungs. The harder she tries, the more irregular her breathing becomes.

"Blackton! Help me! I can't breathe!" She waits for a voice. Instead, she notices a brightness way down the path, catching skylight like a single sparkle on a lonely sea. She paces herself toward it, counting, envisioning two hands, ten fingers, teaching her to count. By the time she reaches the brightness, her breathing has returned to nearly normal. Stooping to pick it up, she wants to yell out, "Jiaré, I have your earring!," but the quiet will not allow such coarse disturbance.

Serves her right for leaving me stranded.

Tanner Blue holds up the earring to the sky like an offering to forces she would like to understand. Its irregular shape is more flat than round, the size of her earlobe. The two varieties of blue match so closely, the outer edge of the earring appears as a small outline against the vastness of the sky. But that is less remarkable than remembering the shade of blue—Aqua Aura. She hooks the earring into the pierced hole of her left ear as the safest place to save it for its owner. Her heart beats signals on the drum of her soul. That rhythm is a simple dance between the steadfast paintbrush in her hand, Blackton, and the unlocked door to her place.

~11~

The large, light-filled room smells sweet, this scent stirred into the yellow-orange walls and floors textured with fine particles like sand. A smooth, curved, off-white table follows the arc of a couch upholstered in quilted fabric. On a counter backed by a long window, several ceramic bowls are filled with small, brightly colored spheres. To the right is space partitioned for sleeping, dressing, and bathing. Latticed doors open onto a backyard that slopes down toward the stream, which is fully wooded on its other side. A yellow house is set back from the bank closest to Tanner Blue's place.

She steps out back, drawn to the trickling sound of water spoken by the stream. It makes her think of sleep and dreaming, causing her to wish she felt tired enough to do some of both. Quietly, she sits beside the water, soon lost in its reflections of sky, leaves, and the house whose door closes swift and smooth as hinges of imagination. That slight movement ripples the stream, spreading an unsteady sensation beneath the surface of Tanner Blue's skin. Her breath grows short, weakening her arms and legs. It requires extra effort to squat first, then stand.

Water. Air and water are her needs. Breathing deeply, she feels better, but this does nothing for the thirst. The water in the stream invites her to drink, but it is much too deep. She sees herself tumbling into it and not knowing what to do, drowning.

Stepping back, Tanner Blue turns toward the yellow house, now covered in shadow caused by turquoise clouds. The sun has stealthily abandoned the sky leaving her thirst behind to multiply. She wipes her lips and tries to swallow. Her mouth and throat are completely dry. A reflex for water drives her to the porch of the house where she balls her fist to knock. The door opens before her knuckles can beat against it.

"No need." A tall man, slender and dark-brown, stands in the doorway.

"Could I trouble you for something to drink—some water? I'm so thirsty."

He points his chin toward the stream.

Tanner Blue turns quickly toward the water and back. "It looks so deep...."

The corners of the man's mouth tense slightly as he nods. "I see. Come in."

Though there is no lock on the door, once the man shuts it, Tanner Blue feels confined despite an incredible openness of interior space. The inside of the house seems a good five times larger than it appears from the outside. Each wall has ample windows but it feels darker than it should. The layout is similar to her place except there is a loft at the top of a spiral staircase. Despite the walls, windows, and the staircase, the dominant material is fabric. Quilts hang from the walls. They decorate upholstered chairs and sofas. Quilting squares clothe the bodies of the man who answered the door as well as the women and men seated at a long, wide table. A quilt is in progress on its surface, each Almáte contributing their part. All at once, as if from one body, they greet her. By the time Tanner Blue returns the customary gesture, the Almáte have resumed their work. A child dressed in a hooded robe with vertical blue and white stripes appears. His skin is light brown. He takes Tanner Blue's hand and leads her to a chair beside an ancient woman seated at the head of the table. The moment Tanner Blue sits down, the brilliant colors, intricate patterns, and vibrancy of the quilting squares bring her to tears.

The child hands her a small cup that has no handle. It feels ceramic, but is transparent. Tanner Blue tilts its brim past her lips. Drinks so deeply that she feels herself drowning and gasps for air.

"Have something to eat." The child takes back the cup and places a blue sphere in her hands.

"What is this?"

"Food."

Tanner Blue takes a bite. It is sweet, salty, and sour on the outside. Inside, it is a creamy orange color with tiny, slightly bitter seeds.

"Is this the only kind?"

The child shakes his head.

"Why did you give me this one?" Tanner Blue holds up what's left.

"Because you're Tanner Blue."

"How do you know my name?"

"We just know."

Tanner Blue looks around the table into sepia faces. Umber, nutmeg, blue-black beautiful. Thoughtful, wise, smiling. A family of fingers works the fabric deftly with copper needles.

"How come I don't know your names?"

The child shrugs. Sits in Tanner Blue's lap and touches her right cheek.

"Name us. Start with me."

He places his other hand on Tanner Blue's left cheek and smiles into her eyes. She wraps an arm around his waist.

"Do you have names, already? You want me to guess them?"

The child shakes his head vigorously. "We don't need them, but you want to call us something, so go ahead. Names will be fun for a change."

"How do you even know what names are then?"

"Because you're used to them. They must be important to you."

All eyes are fixed on Tanner Blue. Most hands are folded, their needlework temporarily abandoned.

She whispers to the child. "Can you help me?"

"Sure. Just reach out. Then, pull some names out of the air."

"You mean that?"

"It's just an idea."

Tanner Blue takes a deep breath. Raises her right hand and grasps at nothing. It is like being under water. She lets her hand fall to her lap. "Never mind. If you don't need names, neither do I."

"You didn't believe it would work. That's why you came up empty handed."

Smiles turn to frowns. Fingers pick up needles that pierce seas of fabric with waves of thread. The room grows cold. Feels dark.

Tanner Blue lifts the child from her lap and stands. She says, "I'm sorry."

Frowns turn to grimaces. The silence is thick, heavy, and hard. Shiny needles moving in and out of cloth catch glints of light from candles, casting paths along the surface of the fabric. Patterns appear—roads, rivers, mountains—all leading somewhere. Tanner Blue is afraid to let her concentration slip away from the story the cloth is trying to tell her. She believes missing the slightest detail would be like losing a thought, unforgiving, refusing to return, but her vision feels as thick as the silence that fills the room. The silence is so heavy it covers up the names of the people who seem to have expectations of her.

To steady herself, she leans forward and flattens both hands on the table. "Do you want something from me?"

They all turn toward 'her place,' visible from one of the windows.

"You want me to leave?"

The man who invited her inside appears.

"We want you to stay, Tanner Blue. We want you to find your place, within 'your place.' But for now, you should get some rest."

Tanner Blue initiates the almáte greeting, relieved that it is returned. The man sees her to the door.

On the short walk to her accommodations, the notion of finding her place within 'her place' tumbles over in her mind so many times she feels as if she is falling downhill while walking up the incline. Midway, she stops. Throws up her hands and talks to the full, daytime moon that emerges from a screen of turquoise clouds.

"I just want to know if it's true. Was I born to be a painter?"

"What is being born?"

"Blackton! I'm so glad you're still here."

"Of course, Tanner Blue. If you're here, so am I, wherever that might be. Now, how about an answer to my question?"

"Being born, it's a beginning."

"Isn't that what you have here?"

"This is different—I'm fully grown."

"Fully?"

"I'm not a newborn."

"You're new here."

"Yes, but no one just gave birth to me."

"And how do you know that?"

"I think I'd remember...."

"Tanner Blue?"

"Yes?"

"Maybe, sometimes you think too much."

"I don't think so."

They laugh.

"I can tell you something, Tanner Blue."

"What's that?"

"This is your home."

She is standing at the front door of her place.

Her feet dangle high above the bottom of the stream. Her body tenses, cramps. She cries out, "I trust you, I don't trust myself. I want us to be friends!" Tears stream down her cheeks, drying the water, turning it solid. Still, she cannot stay afloat.

Tanner Blue tugs at the quilt covering her bed like protection. She means to use it as a shield against the sharp sunlight that invades her room, but the quilt sticks to a corner of the bed. Torn between finishing the dream and extricating herself from its suffocation, she curls up tightly and dives deeper under the covers. She finds a comfortable position except her foot is blocked from stretching out to the edge. At first, she thinks slumbering in her white blouse and jeans could be to blame for this constraint. Propped up on her elbows, she discovers what is in her way.

"Jiaré! I didn't hear you knock."

"I didn't."

"I need some privacy." Fully awake, Tanner Blue sits up and hugs her large, fluffy pillow.

Dressed in pink, Jiaré says, "So, you've decided to stay?"

"*Decided* is a strong word." Tanner Blue looks around. "I'm here. I have to make the best of it."

"How generous of you." Jiaré stands.

"What's wrong?"

"I was hoping you wouldn't be one of those people who doesn't know what to do when they get what they've asked for. I suggest you put packages out of your mind."

"What packages?"

"Expecting what you say you want to look a particular way. Leave some room to discover what else is connected to your dream."

Tanner Blue stands and looks her guest directly in the eyes. "So, Jiaré, you're telling me you went right from A to Z when you first got here?"

"I'm trying to help you use your wisdom."

"When I was a child, I wanted to be wise."

"You've made a good connection."

Tanner Blue touches her left earlobe. "You dropped this when you were busy deserting me."

"How could I have deserted you when I left you that earring?"

"Why didn't you just give it to me?"

"Does it matter? Keep it. You might find it good company."

"If I didn't tell you, I'd be stealing." Tanner Blue notices that Jiaré wears a pair of earrings both of which match the one in her own ear.

Does she have a whole closet of these things?

Jiaré laughs.

"What?"

"I know what you're thinking. Relax. It's obvious from the look on your face. I don't know *all* your thoughts."

"Tell me something, Jiaré. When I first got here, I saw these people crossing the stream. Were some of them leaving?"

"Yes."

"Why?"

"They wanted to stay, but they decided to go back where they came from and spread the word."

"What word?"

"That we are always here."

"Jiaré, they wouldn't talk to me—the Almáte in the place right down from me, closer to the stream."

"They speak through their work. Isn't that what artists do?"

"Who *are* they?"

"The Pathers—the ones who have always been here and have decided to stay. I'm a Doublet, a reminder of the sooner place before birth."

"The *sooner place*? That's what Blackton is?"

"For you. Now, I must know something, Tanner Blue. Why do you paint?"

"It's just an activity."

"But why *that* activity? Say it in one word."

"It doesn't really matter. What matters is you said I have to paint my way back to where I came from, right? Well, let me get started." Tanner Blue takes one step toward the main room. Jiaré places her hands on Tanner Blue's shoulders.

"Your reason makes all the difference in this world. Come on, Tanner Blue. One little word."

"It's not so little, Jiaré."

"Then, one big word."

Tanner Blue sighs, receiving energy from light that streams through the window above her bed. "Connected. Painting makes me feel connected."

"To what?"

"To everything I paint. To everything."

"Then why wouldn't you want to do more of it—why wouldn't you want to feel connected?"

"Because where I come from, that's just not enough."

"I see, but you're here now."

"What about you, Jiaré—why do you paint?"

"It's who I am. It's what I've always done."

"How did you *know*?"

"I never had to ask. Come, now. You've got work to do. The sooner you get started, the sooner you finish, and the faster you can leave. Right?"

"That's right." Tanner Blue gets to the opening between her bedroom and the larger space. Turns around. "I'm just afraid Blackton could be too good to be true—or perhaps, too true to be good."

"Now that just might be the truest thing you've said so far. So, what are you going to paint?"

"I have absolutely no idea."

"When you do, you'll find everything you need in the blue cabinet. You can't miss it."

The two women exchange almátes. Jiaré leaves the front door open, letting in humid, heavy air. Tanner Blue opens the back door and every window. Though air flows more smoothly, it can do nothing to hold back the walls that threaten to close in on her. A blank partition stands before one of them. It is about six feet wide, four feet long, and roughly three inches thick. She tries to move the partition but finds it is rooted to the floor. Walking around to its other side, she trips on a metal handle beneath her right foot. Notices that it is attached to a pale blue sliding door. She squats and opens it with some effort. Inside, compartments are neatly stocked with canvases, sketch pads, tubes of paint. Brushes, cloths, a large water jar. Erasers, pencils, a palette and knife. Crayons. All she could use is an easel. Tanner Blue checks the two closets in her place finding clothes in one—linen and bath towels in the other.

What am I supposed to…?

She faces the partition. Traces her fingers back and forth across its surface. It is smooth in some areas, rougher in others. Tanner Blue makes a mental note to try and let the texture be a natural part of the painting. Changing directions, moving her fingers diagonally, she looks for patterns. Speeding up and slowing down, she envisions a thin outline and does her best to repeat the course of invisible lines that etch themselves into a mural. Standing back, she sees her progress—the areas that are filling in, the ones demanding to stay blank on the surface that presents itself as one large grid of four quadrants.

Ready to commit her vision to pencil, she sketches in shapes—a large square suspended in the northwest quadrant; a long rectangle that extends above the center of the grid; one circle grazes the southeast corner of the rectangle; a vertical band defines the eastern edge. All else is negative space.

She stands back. Tilts her head from side to side, imagines shapes with colors. Green, red, purple. Magenta, yellow, orange. Cobalt blue, ultramarine, periwinkle. Turquoise, teal, lapis. Aquamarine. Tanner Blue. They all swirl into the moisture that fills the room forming walls that shut her in. Tanner Blue drops to the floor. Tucks her knees into her chest. Rocks back and forth. Behind closed eyelids, she dives out, into the stream of life. A self-made music travels through the stream—gentle, bell-like voices guiding sounds of crystals brushing against each other. It is the light that teaches her how to swim except she is outside of water. Air swimming, gliding on the light. Neither bright nor dim, the light rides a breeze through her place, becoming an embrace.

I remember, Tanner Blue. I remember when and why you were born. I was there.

Blackton?

A light breeze blows, feeling like a shrug.

Happy now?

~13~

On the main road, Tanner Blue encounters the man who let her into the Pathers' house. With an almáte, she asks, "Where can I find Jiaré?"

"I can tell you where she lives." He points to an orange place, downhill, to the right.

"Thank you." She smiles and heads in that direction. Instead of bordering the stream, it is canopied by trees that fan the roof with each wispy breeze. At the front door, Tanner Blue cannot bring herself to barge in. She knocks three times.

"Jiaré?"

"Come in, Tanner Blue."

Tanner Blue steps inside this place, which is nearly the same as hers except there is no partition and the walls are green gradations. Jiaré sits at a kitchen table at the back of the house wearing a long, red-orange dress. Her hair is gathered into a short twist that brushes the top of her spine. She motions for Tanner Blue to join her. Pours hot liquid into two cups and hands one to Tanner Blue, who sits across from her.

"Tea?"

Jiaré nods.

Tanner Blue inhales the steam escaping the cup before sipping. "Mmm. Cloves. Some licorice and peppermint. You knew it was me because no one else would knock."

They laugh.

"I've visualized the painting and sketched it out. Tell me that's enough—that I can go back now."

"What's your hurry?"

"I can't live this deep inside my imagination. I thought I could, but I was wrong."

"So, you're sure you're imagining being here."

"I'm not sure of anything, Jiaré."

"Do you trust me, Tanner Blue?"

"I don't think you'd harm me."

"You can make this easy or you can do it the hard way."

"Make what easy? Do what the hard way?"

"Make enough room—just enough. You get to decide how much. Give yourself a real chance to finish something—to know the powers of completion."

"Why is that so important?"

"It's the only way to be whole in the process of growing and learning."

"So, I'm stuck."

"If that's how you choose to see it."

"What have *you* finished?"

Jiaré looks away, her lips half smile, half frown. "I finally finished my own painting."

"Can I see it?"

"It's with the Pathers."

"What are they going to do with it?"

"I'm ready to become a Pather. Since you arrived, I decided I want to stay for good. There's a ceremony — an initiation. You must come so you'll know what to do when it's your turn. Don't say a word — not one. Observe."

"I'm not going back into that place. I felt like an intruder. Let me just get back to my painting. I'll let you know when I'm done. Thanks for the tea." Tanner Blue places her cup in the sink.

"No one stays or leaves without their consent. You might as well get used to them."

"That's not what you said before. So, there is another way."

"There is, when you're ready. You really should come with me, Tanner Blue."

"I'll walk with you, Jiaré, since it's on my way, but that's all."

The return seems quicker than the journey to Jiaré's place. Tanner Blue accompanies Jiaré as far as the meadow that separates her own place from that of the Pathers.

"I hope things go your way, Jiaré."

"You be careful, Tanner Blue." Jiaré glides toward the big yellow house and disappears inside it.

There is slight movement on the other side of the stream. Tanner Blue walks down to the bank and recognizes the man from when she first arrived. Like then, he kneels. Points to where he delivered an object earlier. Looking at the stream, it appears wider and deeper the longer Tanner Blue gives it her full focus.

"You want to leave?" His voice is a strained whisper. She is shocked to hear him speak and understand his language. Despite the distance, he seems near.

Before answering, she is acutely aware of her voice's volume, not wanting to attract any wrong attention. She cups her hands to the sides of her mouth to amplify her reply, "Yes, I do."

"Then come, quickly. I will help you escape."

Tanner Blue rolls up her jeans. She wades in to her ankles, calves, knees, reaching the center of the stream. "I thought it would start out deep. Maybe I can make it all the way across." The current tugs gently and strengthens. Her legs are warm, her feet, cold.

"How deep is this water? Can I drown?"

"You must trust it."

"Oh, I do trust it to be itself. It's myself I don't trust in it."

"Well, whenever you're ready." He turns away.

"Wait! I'm ready!"

"Then, jump in."

"Okay. I'll do that. First, tell me, what is that you placed on the ground there?"

"Come see for yourself. All you have to do is touch it and it will take you back where you came from. I have to go—right now." He waves and soon disappears into a thicket. Free.

"Wait! Not so fast...."

Tanner Blue backs out of the water. Collapses onto the grass and stares across the stream whose calmness slaps her in the face.

What must I do to be your friend?

"Tanner Blue?" Small fingers rest on her left shoulder. She looks up into the eyes of the young boy who was in the Pathers' house and tries to smile at him.

"Do you have a name for me yet?"

"Freeson."

He tilts his head from side to side. "Freeson. Freeson. I like it. I'll tell you a secret."

"What's that?"

"The man who let you into the house is Akúnde and the oldest woman at the table is Almá."

"Why are you telling me?"

He shrugs. "To meet you halfway. Come on inside." He bends over and grabs her hands. "Jiaré's becoming a Pather. They're critiquing her painting."

"*Critiquing?*"

"You know, analyzing it. Letting her know if they think it's done."

"I know what *critiquing* means."

"Come on, Tanner Blue! Come on, come on, come on!" Freeson grabs her arm and pulls her toward the front door.

"Wait." She stops at the threshold. "Are you sure it's okay for me to be there? They probably won't even notice me anyway, right? I'll just sit in a corner."

"They notice everything."

"Freeson, I would have felt much better if you'd lied about that."

"There is no lying here. It's a learned behavior and no one here is interested in anything but the truth."

"A learned behavior...."

Freeson opens the front door and pushes Tanner Blue inside.

~14~

Inside the yellow house, Tanner Blue sits on the floor, hoping she is out of sight. It takes her eyes a while to adjust to the thick and heavy darkness inside this place. The interior feels even larger than before, so vast that beyond her corner, she can see no other walls. When she is able to make out forms, she recognizes the Pathers—ten of them, seated in a circle. Jiaré is at its center, sitting next to a large canvas. Akúnde and Freeson stand together outside the circle. Further be-friended by the darkness, Tanner Blue tries to see the details of the canvas, attempts to understand the words that are being murmured. Her vision stabilizes—the canvas faces away from her.

She does not want to move to see it, preferring to remain un-seen. But each sound uttered by the ones discussing this work ham-mers against the inside of Tanner Blue's brain so insistently that she presses her hands against the sides of her head to muffle the din. The cushions of her fingers intensify the sound until it becomes so loud she does not realize that she is screaming.

The murmurs stop. All eyes turn toward her. She feels like a trapped four-legged, betrayed by darkness that had always been her protection—until now. Tanner Blue wants to run and stay, laugh and cry, die and live. Never has she felt more alive than right now, inside this stirring silence. This place, these people, this moment—they all wait for her. She has done much waiting without knowing. Now, she knows this much. There is only the matter of knowing what she has been waiting for.

No one moves. No sound registers. Tanner Blue breathes harder to break the ice of this thickened silence. Her legs feel stiff. Numb. She must stand or they will fall asleep and turn her into a statue. Pressing the heels of her hands into her knees, feeling doubled in age, she straightens up and gets on her feet. Places one foot in front of the other and reaches out to Freeson, who wraps both arms around her waist.

This place breathes a great sigh that causes Tanner Blue to tremble until she replaces her own shallow breathing with full intakes of air. Her lungs feel sore until she knows they are applauding the new balance that finally prevails.

Murmurs become words that flow from Almá's lips.

"You!" She points at Tanner Blue. "Tell us what *you* see."

Briefly, Tanner Blue places her hands on Freeson's shoulders to steady herself. Releasing him, she plunges into the deep water of the inner circle where she stands beside Jiaré and her painting.

A female form sits cross-legged at the center of the canvas, back to the viewer. Her head tilts slightly to the left—so slightly that Tanner Blue tilts her own head to check that it aligns with the figure. The figure is hairless, wears no clothes. Only the outline of her left breast identifies gender. Her body is different shades of purple and magenta with highlights of green. Three planes define the background. The largest one is mixed-green negative space created from a line that is level with her left shoulder. Elbows rest on knees. The line extending from her folded right knee forms another plane, an extension of the green. The plane beneath her sitting bones is her foundation colored with reflections of her skin. It is the woman's ribs that capture Tanner Blue's attention. She sees them expand and contract, forced in and out by invisible lungs attuned to a pulse that controls Tanner Blue's own breathing. Tanner Blue holds her breath and the figure sits completely still.

Tanner Blue steps back, stumbling on the sandy floor.

"I see a whole life, to that point." She looks at Jiaré, whose eyes are full, shedding tears when she closes them while rocking back and forth, gently.

Almá stands with adolescent vigor. Moves behind her quilted chair. Gracefully places her hands on top of it and says sadly, "It misses inspiration."

Tanner Blue strokes the painting as if she is peeling off dead skin, freeing up the pores to breathe in new and freshened air. She opens her mouth to speak and notices that Jiaré presses her palms together and touches fingers to her own lips. Uncontrolled words gush from Tanner Blue's mouth.

"Can you *feel* all this complexity?

"You don't know who we are, do you?" Almá releases the chair and clasps her hands behind her back.

Tanner Blue glances quickly at Jiaré then back at Almá. "You're the Pathers."

"What do you know about us?"

"Please. Tell me what I should know." Tanner Blue looks for another chair. Freeson brings one to her. She moves it directly in front of Almá and listens.

Head tilted slightly back, as if continuing the motion set forth by the figure in Jiaré's painting, Almá closes her eyes and speaks in a voice one half-octave higher than the one she used before.

"Blackton knew all of us before we were ever born. Knew we would someday and always need to know our way home. Black is not a skinless, sun-less sky. It is a mirror of the endless nighttime ocean. That became my new skin. Love cut off my mother's breath as it called her to the sea. She could not live with herself as it was and could not take me with her. Her chains were not bound to mine. Certain people knew our bond and kept us apart, thinking – no, believing – that a chain is stronger than a link. My mother, she whispered her last hope in my left ear and gripped my shoulders. Then, she transferred all that strength to the railing of the ship. Looking into the eyes of her chain-mates, one by one, at once they all nodded with one mind. Doubled over and slid into the mirror of the endless nighttime sea.

"Nine of them. They formed a circle, holding hands. Rose up high, and sunk way down. Stars formed on the surface of those waters, a path of shooting stars reflected to the sky. I heard my mother's voice:

'Life is a storm. The earth is not our home. They will call you Almá and you will be the Great Mother.'

"I was a child. I knew without understanding. I do not sleep at night because of the echo of that voice. It stays so loud.

"Let me tell you. Let me tell. To be a slave is a mistake but no accident – a reminder of how quick and easy a conscience can be erased, a heart dissolved in blindness to the sight of blood and pain. Ten of us. We call you with our light. We are, and always will be, everywhere."

Almáte.

Akúnde and Freeson help Almá to her chair. She sits so close to Tanner Blue that their knees touch. Though Jiaré's painting is behind Tanner Blue, she feels the skin and bones of that figure's knees jutting outward, rippling energy across the universe.

Tanner Blue leans inward. "*Almá*—Great Mother?"

The elder nods, slow and solemn.

"I'm named after a great painter. I must honor him. Come with me, Almá. Please." She turns around. "Jiaré, you come, too. I must show all of you something in my place."

Like a solid shadow, Jiaré approaches Tanner Blue and Almá. "The Pathers do not go to other houses."

Tanner Blue places her hands on top of Almá's, connecting to her pulse. "Trust me, you'll want to see this."

The nine other Pathers stand firmly at Almá's back. She squints and studies Tanner Blue's face intently. "We will come." Almá heads toward the door, followed by everyone except Jiaré.

"Almá! Why? Why are you making an exception for her?"

"Simple, my dear, like your painting. Tanner Blue is the first one to tell me, herself, that she is ready to do her work."

~15~

It is the presence of the Pathers that makes Tanner Blue realize she has been alone since inhabiting her place. She learned the word, *opposites*, as a young child, *yes* and *no* being the first examples. Before too long, the pairings increased their levels of difficulty, leading toward *easy* and *difficult*, *good* and *bad*, *alone* and *together*.

Together, Tanner Blue and the Pathers examine the sketch she drew on the functional canvas in her place. Muffled words pass excitedly among these guests. Akúnde and Jiaré stand behind them, Freeson in between, inspiring growth through the openness of youth. The other Almáte tilt their heads from side to side, yet uncertain whether they should be pleased, confused, or angered.

Tanner Blue points to her sketch and addresses Almá. "What do you see?"

"This is what I mean by inspiration. It is the design for our next quilt. We have already started it. I have seen it in a dream."

"Almá, Jiaré has been my inspiration. I probably wouldn't have kept painting without her."

"At least my work is original." All eyes turn toward Jiaré.

"Mine is too, Jiaré. I talked with you about it."

"You also told me you thought you were already finished. That you hate being here and want to leave first chance you get."

"I didn't say that."

"You said you wanted to leave."

"I was feeling out of place."

"And now?" Almá places a hand on Tanner Blue's shoulder.

"Now, I have to figure out how this happened—how I could draw an outline of a painting that's the same design as your quilt."

"How do you propose to do that, Tanner Blue?" Almá draws her slightly closer.

"You don't seem at all surprised, Almá. Do you know how this happened?"

"Perhaps."

"Tell me."

"Keep learning the language."

"What language?"

"The one that has nothing to do with names or words." Almá turns to leave.

"Almá. What about Jiaré's painting?"

"I'll give it some more thought." She leaves, followed by the other Pathers. Jiaré, Akúnde, and Freeson stay behind.

Jiaré raises her voice. "Why was that too hard for you?"

"What?"

"Keeping your mouth shut!"

"When Almá asked me what I saw, I was trying to help you."

"I don't need your help, Tanner Blue."

"If I did something wrong, Jiaré, I'm sorry."

Jiaré leaves and slams the door.

Akúnde shakes his head. "That woman...."

"You know how Mama is, Papa."

Tanner Blue studies Freeson. "Why didn't you tell me they were your parents?"

"What difference does it make, now that you know?"

"You're much too young to be so good at answering questions with questions." Tanner Blue smiles, wearily.

"Let's have some food." Freeson takes three colored balls from the bowl in Tanner Blue's kitchen. At her table, they all eat slowly, silently.

Gazing at each guest, she asks, "Do you two know it—this language without words?"

They say nothing, smiling wisely. She begins to understand.

~16~

Between mixing shades of blue, Tanner Blue stops and listens to the music built into each brush stroke she lays down on the canvas. It is only when she has erased the last evidence of white surface that she realizes the music is the sound of her own humming.

Hah! She sits there, before her work, and listens to her laughter. This awareness makes her laugh longer, louder. She cannot stop. All the filled-in shapes on the canvas join her, sloppy-glad in their state of underpainting. Disheveled. Nothing to lose, masters of the world they share with her.

Tanner Blue's mind begins to wander to the colors of the Pathers' quilt. Her imagination tries to grasp those hues, one by one, but she says, "No," and halts the laughter.

No. If the colors, themselves, insist on being the same in paint as they are in cloth, fine, but she will not turn the tide of her own process to one of duplication. Impatient to continue, she blows on the first layer of paint to help it dry. Ridiculous. All too soon, she is out of breath.

Sitting on the floor, she scoots back to contemplate how much detail to add in the next layer. Decides to focus on further defining the square, circle, rectangle—the vertical band and negative space. They wait for her to give them form.

All windows and both doors are wide open, but no air stirs. There is nothing she can do to speed the process. There is nothing she can do but wait and think.

Tanner Blue leans against the jamb of her back door. Looks toward the Pathers' house and the stream. A woman exits the back of the house. Opens a large storage shed and pulls something from it. Climbing the stairs to a side deck, she hangs a red, black, and yellow quilt across the railing. Squares and touching triangles form its pattern. Men, women, and children swim across the water, arriving anxiously at the bank in front of the yellow house. The man Tanner Blue has seen on the distant bank exchanges an almáte with the group and the woman on the deck. Disappears into bushes and mist. The woman looks around and quickly ushers the people inside.

When all is quiet, Tanner Blue approaches the shed. Lifts its lid and looks inside. A quilt with its underside folded out is on top of a heap. She pulls it out to find another beneath it. And another. Nine, altogether. She unfolds each one, discovering distinct patterns unlike the ones in her painting. Different colors, blue missing from all of them.

"You shouldn't be doing that."

Tanner Blue turns around.

"Freeson."

"You're not supposed to touch them. Only the makers should."

"The makers? The Pathers?"

"Yes."

"I shouldn't touch them, either, but I'll help you put them back. Make sure they're in the right order."

"I've mixed them up."

"You should be more careful."

"What difference does it make?"

"You don't think it's important to be careful?"

"That's not what I mean."

"I know. You see that quilt hanging on the railing there?"

"Yes."

"It means something. Each one has its own message."

"What?"

"That's the business of the Pathers."

"Well, let's just put them back. They'll be able to straighten them out, right?"

"Yes, but it can't be a surprise. You wait here. Let me see what I can do."

Tanner Blue begins to fold the quilts, design side out. Soon realizes her mistake. Unfolding them, she notices one that contains ten different patterns—a composite of the others, which individually contain a single, central design. As she gently runs her fingers across each piece of cloth, the squares sing an ancient song of shapes:

Monkey Wrench – Square and small triangles. Gather and prepare.

Wagon Wheel – Circles, funnels, spikes. Pack up your belongings.

Bear's Paw – Squares and claws. Follow the mountain trail.

Crossroads – Four square diamonds. Continue to the City of Hope.

Log Cabin – Square and logs. Know your allies.

Shoofly – Central Square, triangle tips. Free blacks protect fugitives.

Bow Ties — *Squares and touching triangles. You're among friends.*

Flying Geese — *Four stacked triangles. Go north in spring.*

Drunkard's Path — *Large, jagged X. Stagger your movements.*

Stars — *Central square, triangle points. Follow the North Star.*[2]

Tanner Blue uses this master as her guide to replace the quilts, beginning with *Monkey Wrench* and ending with *Stars*. As she puts the last one inside the storage shed, the back door of the house opens. Freeson is joined by the woman who was on the deck before. He opens his mouth to speak, but Tanner Blue intercepts him.

"I'm so sorry to bother both of you. I was feeling a little dizzy, but I'm fine now. *Everything* is fine." She stares hard at Freeson.

The woman sucks her teeth and goes back inside.

Tanner Blue whispers to Freeson, "One of the quilts has all of the patterns. I just used it like a map."

"The sampler."

"Why didn't you just tell me about it?"

"I told you. It's the Pathers' business."

"What's going on inside? Who were the new people?"

"Run-to's."

"*Run-to's?*"

"Yeah, like you. There are all kinds of ways to get here but once you do, you're running to something. I have to get back inside and help the other children."

"Freeson, wait. The quilts — what do they *mean*?"

"They just told you."

She stares hard at the shed. "What do *you* mean?"

"I'll tell you something I don't understand, but I think you might—something I've heard Blackton say: 'Refuge maps its own direction.'"

Once Freeson is gone, Tanner Blue looks in the direction of her place. Runs to it. The first layer of paint on her canvas is perfectly dry.

The second layer of paint lays down easily into five shades of blue. Sapphire square. Lapis rectangle. Aquamarine circle. Turquoise vertical band. Tanner Blue negative space. Everything is in its proper place yet incomplete.

It is the third layer that grits its teeth as Tanner Blue looks the canvas directly in the eye. She reaches that inevitable moment when the nagging question, "How do I finish?," whispers, mumbles, and shouts, letting off just enough steam to leave room for an answer.

Detail.

What are these shapes trying to say? How do they relate to each other? Where did they come from and why did they line up like this instead of some other way? How will I know I'm finished? At least, that answer is always the same. I'll be finished when adding or subtracting anything at all would ruin the whole thing.

Studying the composition, the negative space feels finished to Tanner Blue. It is only the four symmetrical forms that need more work. The urge to copy designs from the other quilts she has seen is great but she knows invention is called for. What can she possibly contribute to the existing body of work that will be more than decoration?

Natural light flickers in the room. Tanner Blue rushes to the back door where she is met by a gentle but persistent breeze. The flickering is encouraged by turquoise clouds drifting across the sky, dodging sunlight, knowing that distance means survival. Other clouds, seduced by heat, get close enough to disappear, but not before drawing a line between wind and sun, a choosing of sides. Shafts of light form a path that lands on the center of the stream like an arrowhead pointing toward what lies beneath the surface. Tanner Blue feels torn by this line of light—how can she choose between wind and sun?

As she returns to her canvas, shadow gives way to light. Colors give way to the powers of their names: Sapphire, Lapis, Aquamarine, Turquoise. How can she transport these forms to the canvas? Perhaps the man by the stream can help. She rushes there, where he waits with clenched fists, separated from her by the stream. One by one, he tosses four small stones to Tanner Blue, waiting for her to catch each of them before sending her another. She carries them to her place where she kneels before the partition and matches each stone with its color on the canvas. Then, she mixes them up— Sapphire to Lapis, Aquamarine to Turquoise—all the varying combinations. It is a puzzle of possibilities. What belongs with what?

Shapes. The stones are different sizes. Tanner Blue sorts them, big to little. Aquamarine is the largest with the most points. Lapis is rough. Turquoise is smooth. Sapphire is half jagged, half slick.

Position. What is the perfect placement for each stone on each shape?

"I see you're making progress."

Tanner Blue looks up. "Akúnde. Tell me what you see."

"I'm not an artist."

"Then what—who are you?"

"A run-to, like everyone else."

"But what is it you *do* here?"

He shrugs. "I just help out when I see help is needed."

"What kind of progress do you see?"

"You stay busy. Some people come here and don't know what to do with themselves."

"How do you help them?"

"I listen—try to make them hear themselves."

"Does that always work?"

"I do my best."

"So, some people fail?"

He shakes his head vigorously. "No one here ever fails. Even if that's what they think, the rest of us are here to hold them up and get them through until thoughts and feelings of failure stop entering their minds."

"Like the reasons some people lie?"

He nods emphatically. "Exactly."

"Akúnde, can you explain something to me?"

"Probably."

"Blackton—I got here through my imagination, right?"

"Go on."

"Why don't I recognize anyone, but you all seem to recognize me?"

"You do recognize us."

"Now, yes, but not at first."

"Did you want to?"

"I guess I wasn't ready to see what—I mean, *who*—was right in front of me."

He smiles. "Continue with your work."

"Is this just a friendly visit?"

"I almost forgot!"

"You *did* forget."

They laugh.

"Almá wants to see you."

"When?"

"Now. Come with me."

"I'm close to finishing the painting. I have to stay."

"This isn't an invitation."

"I can't afford to lose my focus. Almá would go along with that. I'm doing what she said. I'm learning the language of art."

"Listen, I don't think you want me to tell her you said, 'No.'"

Tanner Blue stands closer to him. "Are you *afraid* of her, Akúnde?"

"Yes indeed."

"Why does she want to see me?"

"Didn't say."

"Have you ever seen Almá angry?"

"Once."

"What happened?"

"Everything was lost and we had to start all over again."

"I mean, what caused that?"

"I don't know the whole story, but it had something to do with someone *thinking about* saying, 'No,' to her."

"You're not serious?"

"I'm working on my sense of humor—would you just come with me?"

Tanner Blue looks at her painting. The four stones sitting at its base.

"My concentration is already broken."

"You'll get it back."

"You can never get back to the exact point where you left off. Something's always a little bit different, something you can't know because it's much too subtle the way it gets lost in the shifting of things."

"You know why, Tanner Blue?"

"Tell me."

"Because a new direction was called for."

"You know, I wish I hadn't asked you why you came here. I could have avoided all of this."

"I would have remembered."

"Yeah, but I might have finished the painting by then."

"Then what?"

"That's exactly what I mean. Now, we'll never know."

~18~

Tanner Blue winds up the spiral staircase leading to a loft the size of her entire place. In a corner, facing a large picture window, Almá hums soulfully in her rocking chair. The walls are covered with quilts. Quilt patterns birth from her restless fingers, needle, thread — far beyond the hosting cloth. The underlying material is the finest off-white cotton calling out to former hands that picked, picked, picked away at haunting, harmful color, staining it with blood, reminding black bodies — broken, bent — they were still alive.

Wearily, Tanner Blue rests on the railing, lingers between states of wakefulness, heavily aware of Almá's hands working from their roots. Humidity turns to a heat so fierce that its flaming fingertips close Tanner Blue's eyes, feathering into insinuations on the surface of her skin. They are footprints of slaves perceived through a widening aperture of her third eye with its transparent lid. Tanner Blue eye, looking, seeing forward and back between the worlds. The eye winks. Smiles. Shows off its gentle, convex curves. Closes as Tanner Blue's two eyes open. She glances over at Almá who has stopped rocking in her chair, hands still and folded on her lap.

Slowly, Tanner Blue approaches Almá, mindful that every shut eye ain't 'sleep. It is much cooler by the window, air turned to a chill. Carefully, Tanner Blue lifts the quilt toward Almá's chin. Inhales scents of cotton fields—sweat, blood, dreams. Thoughts have no words, they are like the fleeting footprints of slaves.

"I've sewn more quilts than anyone could count, but the one you're painting, Tanner Blue, it's the first that got started in a dream. None of us would get anywhere without dreams."

"Would you tell me about the dream?" Tanner Blue sits sideways on the windowsill.

"It was the first one I could understand."

"How can that be? You seem so wise—like you know everything."

"I'm just very old. My work as a Pather has been to make a way between the worlds, as if that connection would not exist otherwise. I must now leave room for other ways, like the way you found through your painting. Tanner Blue, you've introduced a whole new way, one where the names—Pathers, Doublets—are no more than names. We are now free to come and go as we please and be more fully ourselves than ever before. Those were the shapes of my dream."

"Does Jiaré know about these changes?"

"I did something I have never done with anyone—I apologized to her. I said her painting 'missed inspiration.' Turns out, I was talking about myself and blaming her for not being you. She still wants to stay and that has been arranged."

"Almá, there are five people I want to bring to Blackton. If we can 'come and go' now, I should be able to 'go and come,' right?"

Tanner Blue laughs. Almá does not.

"That remains to be seen."

"What do you mean, Almá?"

"We can 'come and go' within the laws of Blackton, but once you leave, I can't say whether you'll ever be able to return."

"Almá, do you *want* me to stay?"

"I don't get to want."

As the staircase winds Almá out of Tanner Blue's sight, the sound of each footfall is an echo of stones being tossed into a stream. They tumble, spread out, and settle. Some float to the surface, others are suspended. Colors attach to all of them. Blues. They huddle together to plan their places, break apart and drift a while until they discover exactly where it is that they belong.

~19~

It feels good to walk. Tanner Blue retraces her first steps from the day of her arrival until she reaches that same part of the meadow. She wants to think without asking or answering questions. Her mind gallops under free rein, gliding along the surface of experience, diving into the stream of consciousness it shares with her alone.

She looks around. Sees no one. Listens for the soothing voice of Blackton, which echoes all around her without words. Tanner Blue begins to say something aloud. Stops herself, realizing that impulse was for no good reason, serving only to remind her of the sound of her own voice.

As her mind slows to rest, it settles on a single sensation: peace.

It is possible to think of absolutely nothing.

It is possible to know perfection.

Is it possible to go and come?

Wings flutter and a blue raven lands at her feet. The bird rotates its neck backward and picks through five tail feathers. Plucks one, ambles closer to Tanner Blue and places it before her.

What can I give you in return, raven?

Take me home.

The bird disappears in flight.

"I knew I'd find you here."

Tanner Blue turns. She looks directly at Jiaré and asks, "Are you angry at me?"

Jiaré waves a hand dismissively. "I see now that it was all just part of the package. You've talked with Almá."

"Yes. I have to go back. It would be wrong to keep Blackton all to myself."

"You do know the risk?"

Tanner Blue nods. "I have to try as soon as I finish my painting. I'm almost done."

"Don't get your feelings hurt, Tanner Blue."

"What do you mean?"

"That's all I can say. Just remember those words."

Jiaré walks off, soon falling out of Tanner Blue's sight. As Tanner Blue gazes from Jiaré's vanishing point back to where she, herself, is standing, the blue feather lying at her feet captures her full attention. It feels warm in her hands, softer than it looks and heavier as if made from skin, veins, and blood. Placing it in her pocket, she wishes it could make her fly anywhere she wanted, whenever she pleased. How could that be against Blackton's law?

~20~

The color of each stone matches the hues on the canvas so perfectly that stones and surfaces seem transparent. If only Tanner Blue could lay the canvas flat and see all the stones in clear relationships to each other. Gathering all her strength, she is determined to uproot the partition from the floor so she can have her way. She takes a deep breath, tenses all her muscles, grabs one side of the partition and pulls. It separates from the floor so easily that she loses balance and almost falls. Placing the painting on its back frees up light that brightens every wall in the room. Sitting on the floor, Tanner Blue plays with placement of the stones and watches the puzzle of her work lock down its own positions. In the course of rearranging, a distant bell begins to toll. Its sound grows louder when she moves the stones toward each other, trails off as she separates them. She lets all four stones touch each other, toward the heart of the canvas, and glues them in place. As she inspects her work, the bell transforms into an alarm.

Akúnde rushes in.

"If you're going to leave, you must do it now!"

"I'm finishing my painting."

"It *is* finished. Now, come!"

"How do you know, Akúnde? You said you're not an artist."

"What else could the alarm mean?"

"Plenty of things!"

"I'm *telling* you what it means."

"I'm not leaving until I'm done."

"Fine. Look at it. If you think it needs more work, go ahead. As far as I know, Tolo's the only one who can take people back. Now that things have changed around here, I don't know if he'll be available to Blackton."

"Tolo?"

"The man on the other side of the stream."

"Give me a minute!"

"You've mentioned time. Now you *have* to go!"

"Akúnde, what are my chances of coming back?"

"Chances? You should have thought about that before."

"I haven't had time!"

Akúnde grabs her by the arm and drags her toward the stream where the Almáte are filling up the meadow.

"Tanner Blue, you have to trust me. Would you just walk with me so I can let go of your arm?"

She looks into the face of Freeson's father and loosens her resistance.

"I just have to understand something, especially if there's a chance I won't be able to come back. That alarm—was it to remind me of packages, expectations?"

"Yes!"

"I was expecting a familiar way to know I was finished?"

"Exactly!"

"Does realizing this improve my chance of coming back?"

"Tanner Blue, don't push it."

They arrive at the bank of the stream. The Almáte close in around Tanner Blue.

"I can take it from here, Papa." Freeson stands between Akúnde and Tanner Blue.

"You sure, son?"

"I'm ready, Papa. Come on, Tanner Blue! Follow me!" Freeson runs off. Dives into the stream. His voice becomes her beacon. "Tolo has something for you."

Tanner Blue wades in to her knees, yards from where Freeson treads water. "Keep walking to me, Tanner Blue." Freeson holds out his hand.

She yells hoarsely, "Does the stream drop off?"

"Don't think about that. It's not useful."

Three more steps cover the top of her chest and she starts to tremble.

"I don't know what to do!"

"Dance in the water or think of soaring like a bird. All you have to do is *feel* the water as you move through it." His voice is calm, smoothing out the ripples on the stream. "See yourself stepping up onto the other bank, right where Tolo's waiting for you. See him? I gave him something for you."

She looks and notices Tolo, who waves both hands in the air.

"Freeson, I can do what you say in my head. What about my body?"

He demonstrates his own instructions. When he is almost to the other side, his words drift across the water like notes skipping across a sheet of music: "The water wants to be your friend."

It is twilight. An off-white circle draws its face on the canvas of the rippling stream. The water stills, the sky darkens, shadowed by eclipse. Tanner Blue sees her face reflected next to the sphere.

The moon's still full?

The moon is always full. All you have to do is see through the light.

See through the light...?

Tanner Blue leans forward, her face an inch away from getting wet.

I am your friend.

Tanner Blue shudders, unaware of whether it was she who spoke. She searches the moon's face for lips, finds serenity instead of words.

Blackton? Are you my friend?

Do what the child said.

I wanted to learn how to swim, but there was no one to show me how. You're supposed to relax, right?

Right.

Bracing for cold, Tanner Blue dips her face into the water. Its warmth is soothing like light shed on darkness. She turns her head slightly left then right, standing in place. Slowly, a shaft of light pierces the surface of the water, bending into a path that brightens. She reaches out to touch it, submerging her whole body, panicking as she gropes for something to hold on to.

Oh, no! I need something to touch!

Tanner Blue flails around, trying to make her way back to shore, but a current pushes her toward Freeson, who is standing next to Tolo.

I have to breathe!

Then breathe! Remember what the child knows.

She kicks, screams, takes in water. Lifts her head and fans her arms upward.

Air.

Keep moving. To stay afloat, move just enough — no more no less.

Tanner Blue concentrates on kicking, propelling herself forward, breathing. Above water, all she sees is darkness. Dipping her face back in the stream, the ray of light casts a shining path. She feels its intensity through closed eyes. Her back begins to tense and hurt. She takes a quick breath, does her best to relax, and becomes aware of her own rhythm. At that precise moment, the path dims and she loses her stride. The water channels the trembling that overtakes her body and she begins to sink. Remembering the blue feather in her pocket helps her know the next best thing to soaring is feeling her feet atop the bed of the stream. Wading out clumsily, she collapses on the bank to catch her breath. Her wheezing is the only sound in darkness streaked with moonlight.

"Do you know what this is?" Tolo holds up a flat, rusted piece of metal.

Tanner Blue jumps to her feet.

"I did not mean to startle you."

She looks around. "Where's Freeson?"

Tolo points to the other side of the stream where Freeson stands on the bank and blows her kisses. Hastily, she waves back and then examines the item in Tolo's outstretched hand.

He nods. "Meet Sankofa[3], our memory, our future. Touch it. Hold on to it."

Tanner Blue moves her hand toward the Sankofa bird. Stops short of making contact. "What'll happen?"

"It will do its job so you can do yours."

"Tolo?"

"Hmm?"

"I'm afraid."

His laughter is warm like the stream. "That is natural. Just think about how far you've come, Tanner Blue. We must keep up with Sankofa."

"Tolo, will you wait for me, right here?"

"You are coming back?"

"Yes."

"Hmm." He rubs his cheek. "I was thinking of retiring."

"*Retiring*?!"

"It is my joke. Listen, Tanner Blue, you must embrace Sankofa or I must leave you. I have other work to do."

"Wait, Tolo." She touches his arm. "Just one more thing. Your name, it means something?"

"I am Dogon. It means 'star.' Does your name mean something, Tanner Blue?"

She nods. "It means we must always remember who we are."

Tanner Blue turns her complete attention to Sankofa. Without thinking, she runs her fingers along Sankofa's back and closes her eyes. Breathing deeply, she imagines what it is like to fly.

PART
Three

~21~

Tanner Blue's right fist is numb as if it clenches something precious that disintegrates to sand. A tingling sensation radiates from her fingertips to the soles of her feet, rebounding toward the top of her head. From the ledge outside the window of her shed, a raven lifts off. It aims at the center of a full moon grown pale against gray-blue morning sky.

"Tannerblue." Her head is full of voices. This one feels out of place until she turns toward it.

"Nile? How did you get here?"

He is standing in the doorway of the shed and looks at the path leading to the beach house.

"Walking seemed like the best bet. I suppose I could have projected myself."

"Why did you say that?"

"I meant it as a joke."

"I feel too tired to laugh."

"No wonder. You were up all night. What were you...?" He walks over to her easel. "I see why you're exhausted. Those stones in the center—does that make it mixed media?"

She stands suddenly and examines a painting that could pass as complete. "It's so much smaller."

"Looks like about 36×24-inches, something like that. Maybe it just feels bigger while you're working on it. You know what's strange to me?"

"What?"

"It looks like it took much longer than a night to paint. I can see how you'd lose track of time. Hmm."

"What?"

"Your painting, it reminds me of a flag. Sit tight. I'll be right back." He eases through the door.

Tanner Blue stares at the painting. There is no mistake. It is a replica of the one on the partition in her place. She runs her fingers across the surface and remembers laying down each layer of color. Observing its sides, she realizes that she left all four edges bare. Instinctively, she mixes the right amount of Tanner Blue on her palette and coaxes a wide brush along three outer sides of the canvas, anxious for them to dry so she can also paint the base.

Nile returns, out of breath. "Tannerblue. I've had this book of flags since I was a kid—it was a gift. I've lived so many different spots these past few years, it seems to be hiding from me."

"Who gave it to you?"

"Remember I told you about my pen pal?"

"Freeson." They say his name at the same time.

"Damn, Tannerblue. Nothing's wrong with your memory."

"Nile, what day is it?"

"Sunday."

She rinses off her palette. Washes her hands, dries them quickly, and faces Nile.

"I have to tell you something."

"Can we eat breakfast first?"

"Food. What color...?"

Nile squints at her. Tilts his head to one side. "How about the Lumberjack? I'll drive. That place always tides me over for days."

"Really?"

"No."

Tanner Blue laughs. She lifts her canvas by the back of the frame to avoid disturbing the drying sides. Rotating it clockwise, her jaw tightens and her muscles tense as she witnesses the distortion of her painting turned on its side.

"What's wrong?"

"Nile, does that bother you?"

"They're still shapes. I mean, it makes me feel something I can't explain, but...."

"But what?"

"This way isn't as comfortable."

"Yes, it's unbalanced. You'd think it wouldn't matter because it's abstract, right? But it does."

Tanner Blue rotates the canvas another quarter turn. "Does each turn feel more intense, farther from the center?"

"What center?"

"Balance."

"Tannerblue, truth be told, this is getting a little too deep for me. Maybe I'll be able to follow better after we eat."

"My treat, to pay you back for my birthday. Let me get my wallet."

Nile leads the way toward the house. Tanner Blue lags behind, feeling stuck at the threshold of the shed. Energy is a physical force pulling her in eight directions—east, west, north, south—past, present, future, beyond. She holds on to the door frame to steady herself, prepared to make a choice. The present selects her and she concedes, well aware of its power to penetrate each dimension. Composed but not comfortable, she closes the door, welcoming the necessary sensation of hunger.

~22~

There is no menu at the Lumberjack located on a strip of land called Cargo, thirteen miles south of Tourmaline Beach. You eat what's put before you. More important to the owners than a menu is a laminated information sheet about how its designer did his best to make the diner imitate a redwood log. Strips of rounded bark molded to the façade are a strong reminder that wood comes from trees. At the door, it is easy not to contemplate where wood comes from because excessive amounts of food are the lure. All those calories could translate to enough strength to cut down trees. This is true even if it runs against nature to touch the wooden handle of an axe, swing it hard, trade it in for a chainsaw. Timber, timber, timber. Trees fall like raindrops, crying real tears, landing between lonely footsteps forming through a redwood forest, crowded by trees, creating phobia. Is there a fear of being around too many redwood trees? Is science that specific?

There is nothing scientific about the inside of the diner. It is a warm room with lemon-meringue colored walls. People pour in after church, or they just pour in. A brown sign with large yellow letters in a chrome stand reads, *Wait to Be Seated*. Below those characters, smaller letters say *Please*. The choices are two dining rooms—one family style, the other offers booths with a few leftover tables in its center. Tanner Blue chooses a corner booth.

"It's nice to have your company." She places her hand on Nile's, on top of their table. "I've always come here alone."

He squeezes her hand gently. "My first time here, this brother who was a senior in business management invited as many of us as he could find."

"How many?"

"Five or so."

"That sounds about right." Tanner Blue relaxes into her side of the booth. Folds her hands in her lap. "My first trip here, I didn't know they keep bringing out new dishes, so I made the mistake of getting full on the first round."

"I started to do the same thing, but the folks I was with slowed my roll."

Tanner Blue crosses her legs and her foot hits something. She picks it up—a local newspaper. Spreading it out on the table, she reads the headline aloud:

Hurricane on Saturn Stirs Up More Than Dust

Tanner Blue scans the article. A male server sets down a bowl of scrambled eggs with tomatoes and cheese, another of home fries. A platter with a ham slice, bacon, and sausage. One basket of biscuits, muffins, and rolls. Small coffee pot. Hot water and a mix of herbal and caffeinated teas. Nile loads his plate. Says something Tanner Blue cannot understand because his mouth is full. Seeing the puzzled look on her face, he laughs at himself, chews, swallows, and repeats his words.

"What does it say?" He nods toward the paper.

"Scientists say there's some kind of storm at the south pole of Saturn that's like a hurricane, but the winds are staying still. Most hurricanes form from warm ocean winds but Saturn is all gas, no water. It's the first report of a storm like this on any other planet. Check out this picture of the eye of the storm." She holds up the paper. "It looks human."

"I'm glad there's no pupil. That would be a little too freaky for me. I'm also glad I can't see it blink."

Tanner Blue traces a sentence of the story. "They say Saturn is a very windy planet. Did you know that?"

Nile shakes his head.

"Does it say anything about the rings?"

"There are layers of them, made from ice and dust. Sometimes, it's hard to know what to believe." Tanner Blue sets down the paper. Nods at a black-man and -woman walking through the front door. The man nods back. The woman is a bit aloof.

"You should eat something." Nile puts a little of everything on Tanner Blue's dish. He places a fork in her hand and she picks at her food.

"Tannerblue, what happened to you last night?"

She folds her hands on the table and leans forward.

"Sorry. Eat first. Tea?" He picks one. "This sounds good— cloves, peppermint, licorice. I'll have one, too." He steeps a pair of bags in two large, green mugs of hot water.

"That tea—what's it called?"

He looks at the wrapper. "Just says *CPL*. Looks like they have a variety, but all of the ingredients start with those three letters."

"I've had it before." Wrapping both hands around her mug, Tanner Blue speaks slowly as if trying out a new language. "Nile what would you say if I told you I met him?"

"Who?"

"Freeson."

"There's one sure way to find out." Nile sits back in his chair. Stops eating and wipes his mouth.

"Nile, I met Freeson."

"You met someone *named* Freeson?"

She nods her head. "Yes, but I think I met the same one who used to write to you. He's still a child."

"You know what I'm going to say, right? The same thing anyone else would say."

"It's impossible."

"Correct."

"Did he ever send you a picture of himself?"

"It's inside that book I can't find."

"How about if I describe him to you."

"Go ahead."

"Light skin, curly hair. Soft spoken. I'd say tall for his age but he seemed ageless. They all did."

"Who all?"

"The Pathers, the Doublets. Akúnde, Jiaré. Tolo. Almá."

"Tannerblue, girl, what the *hell* are you talking about?"

"I'm talking about what happened when I sat down to paint. Did you ever send Freeson anything aside from letters?"

He shrugs. "I don't remember."

"Try to remember, Nile. It's important—to me."

"Tannerblue, why are you making such a big deal out of this?"

"I'm just trying to understand some things. Nile, I don't know how I got there, but it was at least as real as where we are right now. I had to swim my way back."

"You're a swimmer?"

"I learned while I was away. I had to. It was the only way to come back."

"So, just where did you go?"

"Blackton. Please don't distract. Did you send Freeson something?"

"*I'm* distracting *you*?"

"Nile, please. What will it hurt?"

He looks toward a display of tea sets by the front door and notices a small gift shop.

"Has that always been here?"

Tanner Blue looks toward the shop. "I think so. Maybe they've remodeled it." She turns back toward Nile. "Why?"

Nile swirls cooling tea in his cup. "I used to go on these bus outings with my grandmother. I think it was part of this church or maybe it was one of those senior citizen's groups." He sinks back into the booth. "Now, which one was it...?"

"Nile...."

"Tannerblue, if I'm going to do this I might as well remember as many details as I can, right?"

"Yes, sorry. Go on."

"I think we just got on a bus one day, or the train. It was the train. We rode north, toward Reno. We got off, I can't remember where—Tracy, maybe. Someplace like that. There was this huge gift shop. Somebody on the train told my grandmother about it. A man. No, this woman. A black couple. I think they had a kid my age or maybe it was a baby. A little girl."

"Sure it wasn't a boy?"

They laugh.

"Yes, I'm sure. She was wearing pink. Anyway, we found it— the gift shop. My grandmother gave me seven dollars—a five, a one, and some change. That, I remember." Nile rests his elbows on the table. "My grandmother picked up every item in the store, but I'm sure she didn't buy a thing. That seven dollars was probably all the extra money she had. She made us some sandwiches. Leftover chicken breasts. We ate one half on the way up and saved the other one for the trip back.

"When I got thirsty on the train, I wanted a soda, but she sent me to get us both some cups of water from the little snack bar. The white-man who worked acted like he owned the train. All I knew was I had to come up with that water for my grandmother. It took me two tries to ask the man for it. It took him forever to get the cups. I would have carried the water in my hands if I could. Finally, he shoved the cups across the counter and most of it spilled. He stood there looking at the mess like he wanted me to clean up after him. I just snatched the cups and hurried back to my grandmother. She asked me why the cups weren't full and I told her the guy was stingy. I hoped she wouldn't ask me to get more. She didn't. It was better to stay thirsty."

"Did you buy something with that five, one, and the change?"

"If I tried, I could probably tell you if it was four quarters, or quarters, dimes, and nickels. How many pennies. I got these two little metal cutouts, I guess you could call them that."

"Why two?"

"I couldn't make up my mind. I think you got a little discount—you know, one is three dollars, but you get two for five. I had two dollars left over. The cashier gave me paper, but I wanted change because it was heavier and felt like more money. I sent one of the cutouts to Freeson."

Tanner Blue holds her breath. "Were they of a bird?"

"I want to say you're guessing, but...."

"But what, Nile?"

"You've *seen* it, the bird I gave Freeson. I mean, that's what you believe, right?"

"Yes, I believe it. Sometimes, believing can make something real."

"But only if it *is* real to begin with. That's what *I* believe."

"Nile, can I tell you everything—will you listen?" She pours him some coffee and adds hot water to her mug.

"I don't even drink this stuff."

"I know that. I wasn't thinking."

"It's about time."

They laugh.

He takes a sip. "Hmm. Tastes good."

"I hope it doesn't make you jittery."

"I have the feeling jitters are no match for what I'm about to hear." He pours in cream and sugar. Holds on tight to the handle. "Ready."

Tanner Blue slides forward in the red tuck-and-roll booth. Her ribs lock against the edge of the redwood table. Aware of her pulse, her veins feel like rings extending the lives of tree trunks, circling Saturn, spinning, whirling, gathering into a third eye, seeing all.

"I simply touched my paintbrush to the canvas and I found myself in this meadow. Jiaré was the first one I met. She took me to my place. It had everything I needed but that wasn't enough for me. Strings were attached, but maybe because I expected strings so something was expected of me. All I had to do was create a painting—just one but it had to be the right one.

"Almá, the elder, told me my painting was the same as a quilt the Pathers were making and the design came to her in a dream."

"Did you ever see the actual quilt?"

Tanner Blue's body goes limp. She shakes her head and looks away. "I took her word for it. Maybe that's what they were working on...."

"Any reason she would lie to you?"

"There is no lying in Blackton. Freeson told me that."

"You mentioned Jiaré. What about the others? Pathlets, Doublers, some other names I never heard."

"Pathers, Doublets, Tolo, Akúnde. Almá. Things start to get a little complicated now."

"Glad I've had a chance to warm up. Hit me." He takes a long sip of coffee.

"The Pathers are quilters. Their work is secretive, but somehow, the patterns in their quilts have always helped us escape. They're permanent residents of Blackton. Doublets travel between Blackton and this dimension.

"Tolo transports people back and forth between this world and Blackton. Akúnde is some kind of helper."

"You and he didn't...."

"Nile, I can't even begin to tell you how irrelevant that seems right now."

"To you."

"I'll respond to that later."

"Now. I won't be able to concentrate on the rest of your story."

"Why do you keep calling it a story? Don't you believe me?"

"I'll respond to that later."

"You've been a good listener, Nile, to this point. Much better than most, I'm sure." Tanner Blue catches the server's attention and asks for the check.

"I can't help the way I am, Tannerblue."

"No reason you should."

"I mean, I won't lie to you, that's a pretty wild experience you had. You have to admit that much."

"I know. I'm trying to do something, Nile."

He pushes his mug aside, flattens his hands on the table and says, "Go on. Tell me the rest."

"I felt closest to Freeson, maybe because of his connection to you. Or, maybe it was just easier to be around a child after my obsession with remembering my own birth. I don't know. He wouldn't tell me his name. In fact..."

"In fact, what?"

"I named him."

Nile sighs. "I'm better now. So, he can't be my pen pal somehow frozen in time."

"I didn't say that."

"I needed to."

"Just because I named him doesn't change anything."

"You said this would get more complicated."

"Freeson coached me on how to swim across the stream to reach Tolo and Sankofa."

"Sankofa?"

"The bird like the one you sent to Freeson. What happened to yours?"

"I keep it inside the back cover of the book he sent me of the flags. So, you swam to the other side of the stream?"

"Yes, and Tolo gave me the Sankofa. It helped me get back here."

"How? Wait. It showed you how to fly."

"I just saw myself flying."

"Then, technically, you should still have the Sankofa, right?"

"That makes logical sense."

"Do you feel like going back to the house and looking for it?"

"I don't mind, but why?"

"I'm just curious. I want to see if it's like the ones I got at that gift shop."

The server places the check on the table. Nile reaches for it, but Tanner Blue's hand lands under his and she pays.

"I like to keep my word."

The male server scoops up her money and his check. A line wraps outside the door like a swarm of termites. Mouths move, weight gets shifted from one foot to the other, people go and come. A cylinder of silence falls over the booth that Tanner Blue and Nile have shared, talking, listening. Wondering. Bowls, platters, and dishes of cold and hardened food have not been cleared from their table. Only now are rivulets of grease obvious, hardening arteries of cracks in the plate still laden with varieties of pork. Tanner Blue tries her best not to wonder whether the server was being courteous in not disturbing their conversation, or if she and Nile are considered part of the debris to be discarded when they are ready to leave.

Tanner Blue raises her voice slightly to be heard above the crowd.

"Nile, can you believe anything I've told you?"

"I don't think you're lying to me."

"You know, I could have stayed in Blackton. Everything was perfect there, but I came back."

"I'm glad you did."

"Nile, I came back for you."

"Baby, my mind just doesn't work that way."

"What way?"

"I can't just make things up."

"So, you don't believe me."

"I didn't say that, Tannerblue." Nile runs his hands over his head. "Who's Tolo?"

"A Dogon. I remember reading they have ancient knowledge of the stars. That's the meaning of his name, 'star.'"

"Listen, baby, I have to get out of here." Nile stands and reaches for her hand. She takes it and says, "I understand."

The server returns with change, which Tanner Blue does not disturb.

~23~

Silver, late afternoon light splashes through the windows of the shed as Tanner Blue checks each surface, lifts and turns over every item on her workbench, and inspects each inch of the walls, door, and window. Her Sankofa guide will not be found.

She leans against the workbench, facing the doorway where Nile stands.

"Maybe it's busy helping someone else. Or, who knows? It could be reuniting with the one inside the back cover of your book."

Nile walks over to her. Holds her face in his hands. "I wish I could be like you. The way you see the world."

"Why?"

"You have a way of making *anything* seem possible."

"But, Nile—it is once we find a way to get outside our minds."

"That's what I mean. I would love to believe that."

"*Nothing* is stopping you." She kisses his hands. Squeezes them and lets them go as she turns toward the window.

He stands beside her. "Baby, what's wrong?"

"I've told you what happened. I have to tell my father. Kali. My mother. And Perla, who gave me a shot at college—we've been out of touch, but I owe her. I have to see everyone face to face."

"What about your job?"

"I have next week off."

On the workbench, Tanner Blue arranges the photos from each parent and the sampler quilt from Kalina as if she is working on a puzzle. She picks up the quilt.

"It all began with this, long before there was a Kalina, you, or me."

Nile focuses on the pictures.

"Tell me about your family, Tannerblue."

"That day we walked the beach...."

"Yesterday?"

Tanner Blue shudders. "Yesterday. You asked me if I'm a daddy's girl. I am. My mother makes me feel like I wasn't supposed to be born. I love her, though, and she has to love me." She picks up the picture her mother sent. "I've never seen any pictures of her with my grandparents. I've seen a few photos of the two of them and they looked so miserable. They never got over the death of my uncle at birth. My mother inherited all that hurt on top of what she must have felt, losing her brother and being blamed for it."

She picks up the picture her father sent. "I wish everyone could feel like part of a family for at least one day. So many people don't even have that."

"I've always had that, Tannerblue. My parents are soul mates and they've always made enough room for me."

"Soul mates. You believe in that?"

"I'm running out of doubts." He kisses her. "I was thinking you were right here all night. Now I feel like you went away."

She kisses him. "I have to go away again, Nile. I could drive to Oakland, but I have so much ground to cover in a short amount of…time." She shakes her head. "The things we convince ourselves are real."

He hugs her. "Like time?"

"Like time." She strokes his chin. "Want to keep me company while I pack?"

"How long's it gonna take?"

They laugh.

"Sure, I'll help. Then I'll run you a nice hot bubble bath, give you a massage, and…."

She relaxes fully into the cradle of his arms. "Could we *and* before that bath or massage?"

"I'll have to think about it. OKAY!"

There is just enough room for them to walk side by side along the path back to the house, arms around each other, creating rhythm. Early evening moonlight glows across the pale blue sky. Seagulls call attention to themselves, squawking about their hunger or perhaps to break the monotony of single-minded survival. Their screeching is like a flashing light in Tanner Blue's head, repeatedly dredging up the word, *soul mates*. Hard as she tries to concentrate on completing the tasks that cascade before her, she cannot catch the color of the flashing light. She is left to wonder if it is yellow, green, or red.

~24~

The North Coast airport is proud of its position, leveled off above the ocean. Willingly, it accepts responsibility for welcoming newcomers, those returning home, and the ones departing. It insists on maintaining a calm atmosphere to fairly represent the lifestyle of its surroundings. Nothing much changes within a wide radius of the runway, control tower, and main building. Ocean, redwoods, and fog are constant companions to each other, reaching out to make new friends because, they have learned, one can never have too many roots.

Awkwardly, Tanner Blue shifts her weight from one foot to the other as she holds both of Nile's hands in hers. They stand before a sign that reads 'Passengers Only Beyond This Point.'

"I'll miss you." He says it. She thinks it.

"I won't even be gone long enough to write."

"It's Monday. You'll be back on Sunday, right?"

"Right."

"Did you reach your dad to let him know you're coming?"

"I did. He's picking me up in Oakland."

"And Kali?"

"I'll call her when I land in New York."

"Your mother?"

"I'll just take a cab. She's about twenty minutes from the airport. What about you, Nile? How does your week look?"

"I've got a paper due and a big test at the end of the week. I have another meeting with my graduate advisor soon as I finish the exam."

"Will you be ready for the test?"

"Yeah. I'm going to study with the Hupa brother in the class. Maybe that sweat lodge he invited me to will help somehow. I was skeptical at first. Now, I'm looking forward to it."

"When's the sweat lodge?"

"All he said was, 'soon.'"

Tanner Blue glances quickly at a clock on the wall. "I'm sorry, Nile, but I'd better get to the gate. You'll have a good week."

"Have a good trip, all of them." He places his hands on her shoulders and stares at the sides of her head. "You're missing an earring."

She removes the blue crystal from her ear lobe. "Keep it for me?"

He takes it. "I'll look around for its mate. Were they expensive?"

"Invaluable, but all I ever had was one. I got it from Jiaré. Nile?"

"Yeah, baby."

"Thanks for not making me feel completely out of my mind."

"I don't know how a person does that but you're welcome." He kisses her once. Two times. Three. Brushes her cheek with his hand. "See you when you get back."

"And I'll see *you* when *I* get back."

They laugh and Tanner Blue breaks away. Her smile diminishes into massive wondering as she approaches the gate, trying to imagine what she will say to her father, Kalina, her mother. Perla. How she will say it. Never before has she tried to convince anyone of anything. Too much responsibility with no guaranteed results. All she knows is she must find a way to make them believe that Blackton exists so they will go there and see it for themselves. If they will not do it firsthand, perhaps they will do it for her so her conscience will be crystal clear.

~25~

Eucalyptus flavors the air outside the small, slate-gray house that holds a father and his full-grown daughter. A deer wanders from across the road into the backyard. Tanner Blue is facing the sliding French doors that lead from the small, square kitchen table where she drinks red chai tea with her father, seated to her right.

"Look, Papi."

Slowly, he twists toward the doors. Laughs and waves. "Hey there, Chester!"

"What if Chester is female?"

"Now, that's none of my business. The color of his fur makes me think of Chestnuts."

"Why not just call him 'Chestnut,' then?"

"Same reason I named you 'Tanner Blue.' It's who you are."

Chester's ears straighten up. He looks in their direction and trots off.

"I guess he doesn't like being talked about behind his back, Papi." She stands and walks over to the sliding door. "Your deck— it's new."

"I told you about it."

"You sure?"

"Hmph. Maybe I just told you in my head. I put it in last month. Chester just got here and look at him. He took off already. Haven't seen him in a while, just like you."

"Last time I came down here was December. You haven't been back to see me since I bought the house three years ago."

"Ever since your mother and me busted up, I like to know what I'm getting myself into. I have no business in a college town around *certain people*."

"*Certain people* aside, do you think about college anymore?"

"I don't have the time. Come, let me show you the deck."

He goes outside and she follows. Tanner Blue runs her fingers along the top of the railing.

"Redwood. Expensive."

"You know Stone. He's always got a deal."

"How is Stone, Papi?"

"You know he and his wife always wanted kids, but never had any. He does have a nephew though, who's helping him a lot with his business. I'd say Stone has never been better. Matter of fact, he's getting ready to retire."

"Next time you talk to him, give him my best, would you?"

"Sure thing, Blue."

"Did he ever see that picture you sent me for my birthday?"

"Don't know about that, but he still remembers what a good time we had that day."

Tanner Blue turns toward the house. "It was hard leaving the house you built for us, but I've always loved this place."

"Seemed like the best of both worlds to me—country and city. I thought it would be good for both of us."

"You were right, Papi."

"You know, Blue, going through that divorce, I felt wrong about everything for the longest."

"I always knew you did the best you could and that was good enough for me."

Tanner Blue looks into her father's eyes and he drapes his arm across her shoulders.

"You know, kiddo, you never know what's going to sink in with a child. I always wanted you to do your best, give your all, and do things the right way. Now, take that deck. I put sealant on it right away and I'll redo it every year so it keeps that nice, rich color." He lets his arm slide to his side. Leans back against the railing and crosses both arms. "Blue, you know where ever I am will always be your home, but I have to wonder—why this sudden visit?'

"Am I keeping you from work?"

He shakes his head. "I've got a small job today. Come with me. We can walk." He opens the hall closet and takes out a brown, canvas bag. Outside, the eucalyptus air is light on Tanner Blue's lungs as she walks beside her father. Each breath cleanses, creating its own balance.

"Here we are." Armande points to a wooden front door.

"Oak?"

"Right-o! I just hung this on Friday. Today, I paint the custom design and do the finishing if the weather's right."

Tanner looks down the road toward her father's house.

"Did you paint your house again, Papi?"

"I'm thinking about it, but it's the same as last December. Maybe something in you has changed."

"That's why I'm here."

"Everything okay, Blue?"

"You tell me after I explain."

"Mind if we talk and paint at the same time? You can help."

"I've always loved going to work with you, Papi. You know that."

He chucks her on the chin. Sets down the bag on the doorstep. "I should tell you something, Blue."

"Okay."

"This house, it belongs to a friend. A lady. She's just been here a few months."

"A close friend?"

"A girlfriend, I guess you could say, or whatever you call it at my age. She travels a lot. Matter of fact, she's out of town for the next few days. I told her I was busy and didn't know when I'd be able to paint the design but really, I want to surprise her."

"Why all the travel?"

"She's a motivational speaker."

"You're not letting her talk you into anything, now, are you Papi?"

They laugh.

"We're taking it nice and slow, Blue, but I've never felt this good in a relationship before, so comfortable with myself. You know?"

Tanner Blue nods. "I can understand. I've been trying to put my finger on what's new about you since you picked me up from the airport. You seem happy."

"I think it's safer to be content, but I won't argue."

"What's the design?"

"She loves pineapples. I did some drawings." He takes them from his back pocket and shows them to his daughter. "How about if one of us paints the bottom part and the other paints the top?"

"Okay. Which part do you want me to do?"

"Let's flip a coin. Heads, top; tails, bottom." Armande presses a silver dollar into his daughter's hand.

"Oh, Papi. It's the one you got the year I was born."

"The very day." He clears his throat. "Go ahead Blue, flip it."

Her voice cracks and she nods. "Okay." She tosses up the warmed coin, catches and uncovers it. "Heads."

Armande takes a pencil and eraser from the canvas bag and begins sketching an outline of a pineapple on the door. "Okay, Blue. Tell me what's on your mind."

"I went to this place where all I had to do was be an artist, a painter. Isn't that what you wanted for me?"

He stops sketching and faces his daughter. "Blue, I just want you to know your own greatness."

"Everyone gets to do that in this place. No one there is like that boss's son, the one at the book bindery. Far from it."

"What's it called?"

"Blackton. Come see it with me?"

"I don't need to see it because I'm content for the first time in my life, right here where I am."

"Is it your neighbor—your girlfriend? Is she stopping you?"

Armande resumes his sketching. "It's too late, Blue. I would have gone in a heartbeat when I was looking to leave New York. Tell you something, though. Since I met Stone and became my own boss, I can think of my very first job, that one you just mentioned, without letting it rule my whole life. Let's talk about you, now. How did you find Blackton?"

"I painted my way there."

"How'd you get back?"

"I swam."

"When did you learn how to swim?"

"I had to, to get back."

"So, you painted your way there and swam back."

"Yes, on my birthday."

He kisses her on the forehead. "Baby, if you did all that in one day, I bet Henry Tanner would be proud. I sure am." He starts painting the bottom of the pineapple.

"Papi, does this conversation feel normal to you?"

"Blue, you've always had a vivid imagination. I love you for it, girl."

"I had to imagine Blackton to make it real, Papi. I want you to imagine it, too."

"I'm trying to tell you, it's not meant for me."

"How do you know if you haven't seen it?"

"Dear heart, I'm trying to tell you I don't *want* to."

"Just tell me Papi, if you wanted to see Blackton, would you say, 'yes,' to me?"

"What kind of question is that?"

"People say 'no' when they want to say 'yes' for all kinds of reasons."

"I'll give you that."

She moves closer so their faces are inches apart. "Would you say, 'Yes'?"

He looks deeply into his daughter's eyes. "Blue, you know that would be my only answer."

Tanner Blue watches her father mix up paint right there on the door. He lays it on so thickly, the texture passes easily for pineapple skin. The red color seems entirely natural to her. She knows the image will feel authentic when the paint dries. Uncertain whether she can match his eye for detail, she thinks ahead to finishing her part. No matter what, she is satisfied that she will have done her best.

~26~

The five-story, red brick building in Greenwich Village sweats stoically with summer heat. It was wintery when Armande brought Tanner Blue here her first and only other time, the end of spring when she was fifteen and he was forty. He made sure they set foot on all the boroughs the few days of their visit.

Her father's age meant nothing to Tanner Blue, then. Now, this distance of ten years whispers in her direction like a gentle tug of war. She plants both feet firmly on the pavement trying not to look like a visitor or worse yet, a tourist, as native New Yorkers pass her by. Slowly, she hauls her blue and green duffel bag up the stairs at the front of Kalina's building. Finds her best friend's name beside the intercom and rings the buzzer.

In half a moment, Kalina rips open the front door.

"Tan!!!"

Girls grown into women, they clamp their arms around each other, then stand back for inspections. Tanner Blue cannot tell if she, herself, feels taller or whether Kalina has lost some height. Kalina's hair is shorter, straighter, and bleached to the color of wheat. A few extra pounds cannot hide beneath a long, off-white, gauze tunic or full, black rayon pants sprinkled with multicolored triangles.

"Kali! It's so good to *see* you. It's been how long?"

"Well, you know Mom comes out to visit me, so I hardly make it to the Coast anymore."

"Kali, it's been ten years! We haven't seen each other since I was visiting Papi and you were visiting your mom at the same time."

"That *can't* be right. How *is* your dad?"

"Never better, doing his own thing. Your mom still vegetarian?"

"Vegan. I see her slowing down, but she stays busy."

A white-man leaves the building. Closes the door quickly after glancing at Kalina and Tanner Blue. Kalina shakes her head, pulls out her key, and opens the door. On the way up to apartment 3-B, Kalina says, "You must be hungry."

"I am. For the first time, I didn't eat any of the airplane food. Don't tell M, you know how she likes to get everything she pays for."

They chuckle.

"You did tell me you're going to see her, right?"

"Yeah."

"Kind of sudden, isn't it, or have you been thinking about it for a while?"

"It's sudden, like my coming to see you."

"Glad you said it."

"You teaching today?"

"Tuesdays tend to be slow. I'm subbing for the rest of the summer. If they were going to call me, they would have done it by now. I start full time at Gunther this fall. Here we are." Kalina opens her front door. "Have a seat. Over there, by the window. Nice view of the trees. Sometimes there's a breeze. I'll start lunch."

Tanner Blue obliges. Places her bag on the floor. Rests her chin on crossed arms and anchors them on the windowsill. Below, a white-child walks a brown dog as a black-nanny looks on. Tanner Blue wonders if she has children of her own, and if she does, who looks after them? Perhaps some kind and caring teacher, as she imagines Kalina to be, who feeds their potential with a spoon of stainless steel. Or, is that child swallowed up in an overcrowded classroom and is their name treated like a number?

"Come, Tan."

Kalina stands at the small, rectangular table in the center of her one-bedroom apartment and Tanner Blue joins her.

"Chicken salad?"

"I remember how much you love it. A little arugula salad and some lemonade."

Tanner Blue sits. She loads her fork and takes a taste. "Thanks, Kali. Yours is still the best. Is the skinny part of chicken wings still your favorite?"

"Yep."

"I always felt a little greedy when we traded and I ended up with more meat than you."

"I got even when you let me have the crust when we got pizza."

They eat in a dinette surrounded by a symphony of fans—one with cane blades that whirs above them, and two in separate corners across the room. The U-shaped kitchen is slightly larger than the dinette, occupying the same basic space. Tanner Blue slips off her san-

dals beneath the table and slides her feet along the smooth, hardwood floor.

"Nice place."

"It's cozy. That sofa's pretty comfortable to sleep on." She
points her chin toward an east-facing wall where a burnt-orange,
corduroy couch seems quite at home against a lime-colored wall.
Several bookcases, a modest music center, and a framed poster of a
sunset take up the opposite wall. A healthy ficus tree stands beside
the bedroom door.

"Um, um, um. This sure does hit the spot."

"I made it last night. Tastes much better today."

Tanner Blue stops eating. "I've been thinking about what you
said, about how I don't give people a chance to know me. Kali, why
do you think that is?"

"You're asking, so I'll tell you. I think your greatest fear is being misunderstood and not listened to because it's happened to you
so much, Tan. It's hard for most people to take chances."

"I'm taking a chance, Kali."

Kalina stops eating.

"Nile and me—we're more than roommates."

"Since when?"

"My birthday."

"Was it a good present?"

"The best one of its kind."

They snicker.

"Tan, you don't know how much I want you to be happy."

"Papi says it's better to be content and that's what I want for you. Will I get to meet Victor on this trip?"

Kalina wipes her mouth and pushes her plate away. "Not if you have to leave tomorrow. He spends Tuesday nights with his parents in Jersey. No exceptions."

"This is the first time you've mentioned that."

"I've been trying not to let it bother me."

"Do you ever go with him? I'm sorry if I'm disturbing a routine."

"No. You're not disturbing anything. I'm glad you're here."

"Good. Has it always been like that?"

"Not when we first got together about a year ago."

"You've met his parents?"

"They aren't crazy about me, especially his mother."

"So, is he going to keep up the Tuesday night visits after you get married?"

"I don't know."

"Listen, Kali, we just talked the other day, right?"

"Your birthday."

"What's changed? You were so ecstatic."

"We told his parents our news the night of your birthday. Let's just say they weren't enthusiastic."

"How's Victor handling that? Does he think they'll come around?"

"He's never known either of them to change. I really love him, Tan."

"And he loves you?"

"I know he does, but his mother has a hold on him. I told him it's not like he has to choose, but he feels caught right in the middle. He's not ready to set a date."

"Oh. How old is he?"

"Twenty-nine. Our birthdays are the same day."

"September 7th."

Kalina nods. "The day I start my new job. Tan, I know you've just been thirty for a couple of days, but do you feel different? I'm starting to feel like it's more than a notion."

"Everything feels different, Kali. Everything *is* different."

"How was your birthday?"

"That's what I've come to tell you about."

Kalina squeezes her best friend's hand. "It's *so* good to see you, Tan! Now, tell me all about your birthday."

"I'm painting again."

"It's about time!"

"Actually, it's not about time at all, Kali."

"Huh?"

"Kali, have you ever been so deeply wrapped up in doing something that you lost sense of time, you lost sense of everything, that you tapped into a whole new kind of sense that meant everything to you, that you couldn't explain to someone else, but it felt so good you wanted to share it with everyone you love? Have you ever felt yourself living outside of time?"

Kalina sits back, staring into space.

"When Victor and I first got together, we flew to Chicago for a weekend to visit some friends of his who have a place on Lake

Michigan. That was the clearest time I felt like what I do day to day didn't exist. I mean, I was so happy, so…euphoric, I had the sense, wow, what if things could always be like this."

"Exactly!"

"Why are you asking me this? What's happened to you since your birthday?"

"Kali, life can be just like that."

"How? I mean, if it can, why isn't it?"

"Because we convince ourselves that it can't."

"And how do you know this?"

"Because I've *seen* it, Kali. I've *lived* it."

"Explain it to me."

"Kali, why did you send me those quilting squares?"

"Good! You got them. They reminded me of your paper towel designs. I thought they might be good inspiration."

"You were absolutely right, Kali."

"I enjoy being right."

They laugh.

"Kali, the moment I picked up a paintbrush and touched it to the canvas I was taken off somewhere."

"Oh, now I understand what you were saying, before. You got completely absorbed. I guess I feel that way when I read a good book and have some new insight into it. I do love teaching. Is that what you mean?"

"It's not for me to say. It's what *you* feel, what *you* mean."

"Tan, I know you're an artist, but can you be a little more concrete?"

"I'll try. First, tell me. Have you seen that woman anymore, the one you bought the quilting squares from?"

"I've been so distracted, I haven't noticed."

"Can we go see if she happens to be there today?"

"This heat might kick your ass, but okay."

Crossing the Avenue of the Americas at West 8th Street feels like wading through murky water. The air favors the west side of the street, the one closest to the Hudson river. Crowds of people move in more than eight directions. Perhaps it is the contrast of their frantic speeds to the sluggish progress of taxicabs, buses, and trucks that makes the hoards feel heavier than usual. By the time Tanner Blue and Kalina reach the other side of the avenue, Tanner Blue is fully exhausted.

"Whew! Did it take you long to get used to this humidity?"

"It's in my Caribbean blood, Tan."

"It should be in mine, too. I was fine until you mentioned the heat."

"Sorry. Do you want to go back inside?"

"I just need to catch my breath. Which way're we going?"

Kalina points south. "Right over there, by the chess players and the basketball court. Why don't you try and find someplace to sit. I'll go get us some cold drinks. Be right back."

Tanner Blue paces down the avenue. Voices and languages stream past her ears so quickly that the noise becomes too loud. So loud that in the spirit of this competition, four clear and simple words prevail: "Come, sit by me."

Sit? Tanner Blue looks around. *There is no place to...."*

An old woman is seated at a chessboard. She looks directly at Tanner Blue and motions toward the narrow bench that is a companion to her own.

"I don't play."

"Maybe I can still teach you something."

Fatigue gets the best of Tanner Blue so she accepts this invitation.

The woman spreads both hands on the chessboard and says, "It's nothing but a mess of squares. You any good at patterns?"

"Patterns?" Tanner Blue examines the chessboard.

"Making sense of them."

"Can I ask you something?"

"Get past the quilting squares. Look at what's right in front of you."

Tanner Blue obeys.

"Where are the pieces? You know, the knight, rook, bishop, king, queen. The pawns."

The woman looks around. "This is a whole new game. Keep looking."

Tanner Blue resists the reflex of counting the squares because she knows that is not the point. Instead, she traces all four corners of the board, then walks her fingers in circles, diagonals. Straight lines.

"No matter what I do, they stay connected."

"Connected to what?"

Tanner Blue's hands rest flat at the center of the board. *"Who —* me."

"Tan."

She turns around. Kalina hands her a clear, full cup.

"Apple-strawberry juice, your old favorite. Were you saying something?"

"I was just talking to...." She turns back to the board as Kalina slips onto the empty bench across from her.

"She sure looked like Almá."

"Who?"

"I saw the woman you bought my sampler quilt from."

"She told you her name?"

"I know her."

"Cool. You know, Tan, I think this heat is too much for you. Come on. Let's go back to my place." Kalina stands.

Tanner Blue drinks half of her juice all at once.

"Actually, Kali, I feel fine. A walk would do me good."

"You sure?"

Tanner Blue nods and gets to her feet. They head east, toward Washington Square Park.

"Go ahead, Tan. Finish what you were telling me."

"I'd like you to come somewhere with me."

"Where?"

"Blackton."

"I like the name. Is it far?"

"There's no place closer. All you have to do is want to see it, agree to come, and leave the rest to me. Kali, it's *perfect*!"

"You know what they say about things that sound too good to be true."

"That's what I thought. Like you and the rest of the world, I like to be right, but I was wrong. A place like that exists."

"You know what they say about timing, Tan. Everything I've been working toward is right there in front me. *That's* what I want to see and finally, I do. Maybe I can come during one of my breaks from school. I could meet you there."

Tanner Blue smiles absentmindedly. "We'll see."

They cross over to the park, which is trafficked by dogs and their walkers, more black-nannies and white-children. Joggers. Students. On a patch of brownish grass marked with a 'Keep Off' sign, a juggler keeps dropping the three billiard balls that go up, crashing all the way down, forming a queue in the gutter.

Kalina nods surreptitiously toward the juggler and whispers to Tanner Blue, "He'd have more luck with something lighter."

Tanner Blue hugs her friend and thinks, *All he can do is try.*

The Caribbean sea looks warm, the cool blues mixed with green and turquoise hints of lavender stir up their own heat. It is all right there in the distance, just beyond the cantaloupe colored front door of the lemon yellow house that interrupts Tanner Blue's reunion with her mother. The amber sun arches toward the horizon. Having traveled so far, it is only now that Tanner Blue tries to think of what to say. The door flies open.

"So, why you come now, child?"

"Hello, Mother. The letter you sent with your picture. You invited me, remember?"

"But this is so sudden."

"You've made at least one sudden move yourself, remember?"

"So much talk about memory and you just got here. Hug me."

Tanner Blue sets down her bag and folds her arms around her mother's back. Her own bones feel so rigid, they creak.

"Come in and sit down. That's a long trip. You must be weary. I'll fix some food."

Soon, two plates of cou cou heaped with stewed flying fish appear on the rectangular table spread with a white lace table cloth. The place is mostly one large, tidy room with windows embracing a view of the sea.

"I've watched you make cou cou plenty of times, but I've never tried making it myself."

"You just boil the okra, be sure to keep the water, and turn it into the cornmeal until it's all nice and smooth. That's the hardest part. Getting it nice and smooth. Lumpy cou cou will give you the worst case of indigestion. You going to answer my question sometime?"

"Why I've come?"

"Yes, that."

"I wanted to see how you are."

"It's been an uphill climb, but I'm making my own way."

"I thought your relatives asked you to come and help."

"Tsck. Child, people only think they know what they want. They never expected me to actually come! Only since I've been making some good cash am I worth something. Can't blame them. How nice for me to be able to pick up and come here just because I felt like it, huh? But I tell you, child, I did not expect them to welcome me with wide, wide arms. I was not at all disappointed because..."

"Because what?"

"Sometimes I talk too much."

"Because what?"

"Because that kind of reception, it had not been my experience."

"What about Papi? Didn't he welcome you with wide, wide arms?"

"Listen, child. I have no cross words about Armande as your father, but you have always acted as if his side of the story is the only one. That man wanted me to depend on him. I tried for as long as I could, even though I was working at a good job."

"What do you mean?"

"He always thought he knew what was best for me without even asking."

"Give me an example."

"He found out about the job at the bank and told me to apply for it."

"I thought you liked your job."

"Child, *like* had nothing to do with it. He likes the house building. All I wanted was a little time to at least think about what I did like, what I wanted to do."

"You told him?"

"Tsck. What for?"

"So he'd know, so you could discuss it and figure out a way...."

"Figure out a way to what, to not pay the rent on time, buy food, and clothes? I was glad to get that job. So, in that sense, he was right. Now, listen. It's good to see you, child, but I was not born yesterday. Aside from 'knowing how I am,' what else brings you here so fast? The ink is barely dry on my letter."

"I wanted to see if we could talk. I might be going away for a while."

"Away, where? What about your job?"

"I've found a place where I can make a living as a painter."

"What kind of painter?"

"An artist."

"You still blame me for those words?"

"No, I don't. That's not why I'm here. I'd like us to know each other."

"You going to sell your house? It's appreciated since you bought it?"

"It's not that kind of transaction."

"Then what kind of transaction it is?"

Tanner Blue smiles.

"My question is amusing?"

"I'm just noticing your accent."

"It's always been there. You just never listened for it before. Maybe it's stronger since I'm back. You want all kinds of information, but you're not all that forthcoming yourself, you know."

"You're right. I discovered this place through painting. It exists in another world, on another plane, a different dimension."

"You think I can't grasp that concept, right?"

"Can you?"

"Child, you know what a *duppy* is?"

Tanner Blue shakes her head.

"So I know something new? It's an impish kind of spirit that plays tricks on the mind, but they are real. I follow perfectly well what you're telling me. What is the name of this place?"

"Blackton."

"They sell houses, or is that kind of *transaction* irrelevant?"

"I don't know yet. Nile, my…friend tells me all I did was stay up all night and paint. It's a place without time."

"It can be like that here in a sense, you know. Things get done on their own terms. Nile, you're serious about him?"

"We're just getting to know each other."

"I have no advice for you, but...."

"But what, Mother?"

"I just hope something."

"Tell me."

"You're still a good listener. Listen to your first mind, child."

"I didn't know you saw me that way."

"We never know all of what people see."

Tanner Blue shifts her weight in her chair. "So, do you have a...companion?"

"I look that old to you?"

They laugh.

"A boyfriend, a partner, a man! Do you have one?"

"Tsck. I hear from someone in the States every now and then. I don't know if I should tell you this. It might be upsetting."

"Go ahead. What ever it is, I'm grown."

"It's not that bad. We both worked at the bank and he was also married. He's gotten a divorce and he's talking about coming here to visit. Be clear, child, I'm talking about a harmless attraction. That's all it was. I was always faithful to your father and I never doubted him that way either."

Marguerite stands suddenly. "I can't sit still for very long anymore. It brings on old age too fast. You're here just a few days and I want to show you all I can about this part of what you come from. We'll go up to Eracra to the hotel for their dinner buffet. I know we just ate. Splash some water on your face and let's go. To-morrow, you can come see where I work in Calichi. Friday night we'll go to Surries for the fresh fish. Saturday, I'm having a little luncheon here so you can meet your relatives. Sunday, you're back to the States. Come, let me show you where everything is."

"Mum?"

"Um?"

"I don't remember you being so…energetic."

"I've always been this way. The only difference is, now and here, I am myself."

"I'll get ready."

"Good. We're agreeing on something already."

They laugh in ripples like the tide that flows outside—an ef-fect that lasts long enough for Tanner Blue to wash her face. She hopes to do some exploring on her own. It does not occur to her to express this presumption to her mother. Tanner Blue would not hurt this woman for the world.

Three white kiosks form the first loose barrier to Cragstone beach. At one, loud, floral dresses are hung on pegs, rippling like flags at the slightest suggestion of a tradewind. All sizes of scarves are neatly folded on display. Another kiosk specializes in jewelry made from beads and shells. It is the third that captures Tanner Blue's attention. Amid sunglasses, visors, and tee-shirts, she finds an 8×11-inch cloth-bound journal that is the colors of the sea. She chooses several ball-point pens with blue, green, and purple ink. A pretty, pleasant, woman around her own age holds out her hand. Tanner Blue pays her and wonders if the woman envies those who can afford to travel far on holiday.

The second gateway to the beach is a cluster of food stands and a bar dispensing rum punch, *Cuba libres*, and *piña coladas*. Tanner Blue finds a fruit juice stand and gets a large coconut milk, fresh in its shell. On the open beach, she rents a chair and umbrella from a fast-talking, slow-moving man who wipes the chair spotless with a clean towel and dusts sand from the umbrella with a whiskbroom. His white, starched shorts are baggy, announcing the smoothened beauty of his blue-black skin.

"They trying to make the beaches here all private so nothing black can soil all this pretty white, white sand. 'Round here, they always poking your eyes out then give you a black stick to walk with. And what you think?"

Tanner Blue shakes her head. "That's not right. How much do I owe you?"

"Four dollars."

She gives him six and he politely kisses her hand.

They poke your eyes out and give you a black stick to walk with.

She does not want this to be the first entry in her new journal, but it insists. Tanner Blue has been to parts of the island where hotels post invisible "Whites Only" signs, which she ignored. Found herself stared at by sunburned faces challenging the audacity of her presence outside the capacity of catering to their whims. Those charged with that responsibility also resented her interjection into their status quo. How many ways were there to be an outsider?

As Tanner Blue's gaze lifts from the page, the murmur of breaking waves, the constant blending of watery shades of blue, green, and foam, and the flow of the tide calm her down completely. The past few days, she has been so aware of pacing herself that now, it is a triumph to be alone and revel in the glory of her own stillness. But not for long. Soon, she creates her own movement by making a portrait of the ocean with her new pens. At first, the thin lines seem ineffective but as their numbers grow on the page, and as they form organic shapes, a likeness of the scene before her emerges. Satisfied with this exercise, Tanner Blue turns the page and starts to write:

Eracra is on the northeastern shore of the island. Shortly after getting out of the car, my mother and I crossed paths with a woman who told us a railroad used to run through there. Mum did not believe her. She would not admit the possibility that no one ever bothered to mention it in her presence. She could not admit forgetting something that big and mobile. We ate at the hotel overlooking the ocean and fishing boats, all different colors. The food was good, different kinds of fried fish, stewed chicken and beef, potatoes, rice. Cakes and pies. No green vegetables. Mum wanted me to eat more, but truthfully, I was still full from the wonderful cou cou she made when I first arrived.

Jet lag got the best of me by the time we returned to Mum's house. I went straight to bed and wanted to sleep, but there was this high-pitched sound, louder and sharper than crickets. It soon became music and I fell asleep. The next morning, on the way to see where Mum works, she told me the sound was the song of whistling frogs.

Calichi, the capital, is built around a harbor. I was expecting to see more people in her office since I had this picture of a family business. The only other person there was Rutherford, my grandfather's nephew. After looking at some pictures of properties tacked to a cork board, I excused myself to walk around the harbor. Parts of the place reminded me of a big flea market. A bar here, a restaurant, there. A market, department store, and bookstore. I went in there and asked about books by Antillian writers and about island history. I was expecting a big section with too many choices, but the woman working in the store had to put some effort into finding at least one of each and I bought both. I went back to Mum's office and she wasn't there. Rutherford said she looked for me to say she had to tend to some business. I left him to his work and went next door to a restaurant and ordered some tasty appetizers. I walked over to the edge of town where a cruise ship was docked, cutting into an outline of sky like the first piece of a puzzle. I passed a lot of the disembarked passengers, women dressed in pink, tan, and white, bringing to mind the color of their skin. They walked with men in beige Bermuda shorts, hurrying to see as much of the island as possible, perhaps to sound like experts when they returned home. Most of them seemed much too preoccupied to notice me. The moment of that thought, a couple shyly approached. The woman asked, "Please don't be offended but could we take your picture? Of all the stops we've made on the ship, we've been most excited about seeing your island."

I asked them, "Where are you from?"

The man, a bit anxious, said, "Your English — no trace of an accent! We're from California."

And I replied, "So am I. Excuse me."

Blue-green letters just beneath the bow of the ship spelled 'Atlantis.' Any interest I had in tourists and the immensity of the vessel surrendered itself to a small, gray boat docked up shore. I walked toward it, soon noticing a man seated on a bollard, looking out to sea.

I looked from him, out to sea, and to the boat. The word, 'Fonio' was hand-painted in red across the bow. When I said it out loud, he told me it was the word for the tiniest seed in the universe, in the language of the Dogon of Mali. It's actually a grass seed for one of their most important crops. He told me they live by their connection to the stars Sirius A, B, and C. Explained how the Dogon knew of Sirius A before western astronomers. How B (also known as Digitaria) is invisible to the eye and considered the place of origin of all beings, and C (also known as Yemme Ya), is yet to be verified by western scientists. Then he talked about how the Dogon have been doubted and how it made perfect sense to him, personally, that if they were right about the stars they probably knew what they were talking about as far as their own origins. He invited me to sit down on the bollard next to him and share a fruit salad. I did. Not wanting to assume anything, I asked if the boat was his. It was. He said the other name for 'fonio' is 'po tolo.' That's the Dogon nickname for Sirius B because it's tiny, yet extremely dense. When I told him a man named Tolo was responsible for my learning how to swim, he said he hoped I appreciated the power of names. Before I could ask his, he stood and said, "Stay in touch."

On the way back to Mum's that evening, I asked her if most of the property sales were to residents or people from other places, *like the tourists who come and go on cruise ships. She muttered something about vacation homes. I asked how many of her clients were black, whether Antillians, from the States, or other places. She said she didn't keep track of such things because they were a waste of time.*

The next day, Geneitha, a retired friend of Mum's took me to a botanical garden, a nature preserve, some caves, and a few beaches. The ones on the west shore are much calmer than the ones in the east. I like the wilder ones, like Cragstone. That evening, the three of us went to Surries for fresh fish. It's right at the water's edge. In the darkness, the boats bob restlessly, waiting for daylight. It was all so lively. There were tables of brightly colored ceramic bowls, dyed fabrics, tee shirts, recorded music, and wood carvings of animals.

Earlier today, I saw Rutherford and Geneitha again. They came to Mum's luncheon along with distant relatives named Ardeline, Eldred, Kelby, Olvin, Leota, Bellfield, Thelia, Winnifred, Cyrus, and Darius. Everyone was gracious and made me feel at home.

And now I'm here. The sky is still bright, hanging heavily over the sea. It's the clouds that give sea and sky their weight. Reflections. I try to imagine what it would be like to live here. I don't know if I could ever get used to driving on the left side of the road.

~28~

The yellow-bodied airplane nests safely on the tarmac and a group of passengers applaud. This sudden noise turns Tanner Blue's head from her view above the sky-blue wing. Studying the cabin, she remembers arriving on the North Coast of California toward the end of her adolescence. Once inside the terminal, the first thing she did was call Perla Magena, who had saved a place for her at the college. Now, Tanner Blue will call Perla again, not to ask for something from her, but to offer something valuable in return.

"Perla, this is Tanner Blue Baptiste—remember? Are you right in the middle of something?"

"Tanner?"

"Yes. Sorry. I know it's been a while."

"Thought I'd see how it feels to take a Sunday off."

"I hope that means you're being as good to yourself as you are to everyone else."

"You know, I'm trying hard to understand what that means."

"I just got back into town, Perla, and I'd like to see you. Do you have some time this afternoon?"

"Where are you?"

"Baggage claim."

"Need a ride?"

"I got in early. My friend's picking me up, but I called you first."

"Listen. There's this new café at the airport. We can meet there. I'll take you home. Save your friend a trip."

"What about your day off?"

"I wouldn't want to rush into that."

They laugh.

"Then it'll be my treat, Perla. For a change, I hope I can do something for you."

"Some of us are slow to change, Tanner. I'll be there in thirty minutes."

Tanner Blue calls Nile. Tells him Perla will bring her home later in the day. Her bag shows up early on the carousel and she stores it in a nearby locker.

The new café would have been easy enough to find without all the signs announcing it, right up to the yellow neon letters spelling, *Café Unique*. Its western border is all plate glass, overlooking a blue-lit runway that stretches toward the ocean. In the distance, a band of junipers lines the freeway. A green jet curves west along the tarmac, stopping briefly before jogging, running, taking off, lifting upward and away.

Beside the cash register, a blackboard is propped on an easel. Green and pink chalk letters describe an array of soups, sandwiches, salads, and desserts. Tanner Blue hopes Perla is hungry, wanting to eat in good company. The café is filling up. As she begins to look for a table she notices her friend approaching.

Perla Magena cannot be rushed. Her long, mauve dress makes it seem as if she glides instead of walks. While Perla does not appear to measure her own steps, Tanner Blue resists the temptation to count. Instead, she marvels at the graceful way her friend moves through the world. Her face is the same harvest moon as always, seeming to light her way. Parted down the middle, her hair is thick—black, interwoven with silver threads. She is solid, built closer to the ground than Tanner Blue.

The two women embrace at the entrance to the café, then stand still, holding hands and swinging each other's arms.

"Perla! Thanks for meeting me today. What can I get you?"

"Same as you. I'll grab us that table by the window."

A line has formed at the counter giving Tanner Blue an opportunity to decide on tomato basil soup, *insalata mixta*, fresh baked *pain levain*, and carrot juice. She pays, grabs a marker for order number 23, and joins her friend.

At their table, Tanner Blue looks around. "I've been trying to figure it out—what's unique about this café. It's the cups. Each one is distinct. They're beautiful."

"I know."

"You've been here before?"

"Many times to meet with the owners. The cups are part of a ceramics program on the reservation. I helped set it up. My mother is black, but my father is Hupa."

"I knew that, right?"

"It's possible I never told you. I lost my connection with the reservation for a long while. The college kept approaching me about doing programs and when the ceramics idea came along, I took it as a sign."

"Of what?"

"I used to love ceramics—the feeling of clay on my hands, under my fingernails especially, like it was in my blood. I had a mentor who just went away. That was when I learned how important it was to have someone take you under their wing. This opportunity was a sign for me to spread my own wings again."

"You designed the cups?"

"The first ones. Now, others are getting involved."

"Perla, you'll always find your way."

"You're the first one to put it to me like that."

A plane lands and taxies south, toward the terminal. Tanner Blue has the sensation that she is just now arriving, that she has imagined Perla's words rather than having heard them spoken aloud. The food arrives and they begin to eat.

"I want to ask you something, Perla. It's not easy."

"Sounds necessary."

"Did I disappoint you, my not finishing college?"

"I would be a hypocrite—I never graduated, either."

"But I promised you."

"Correction. I tried to *make* you promise—for your own good. Is that why you wanted to see me?"

"Not at all. At least, that wasn't on my mind when I called."

"Then, what?"

"Travel. I went to see my father in Oakland, my best friend Kali in New York, and my mother in Antilla. But before all that, I went to Blackton. In a way, it's how I imagine a reservation."

Perla pushes her plate and bowl aside. Wipes her mouth with a pale-green paper napkin. "I haven't heard of Blackton, but I have decided to move back to the reservation. Some family's still there. We might want to start our own café or something, you know?"

"I can imagine."

"Why did you want to see me, Tanner?"

"Just to see you, Perla."

"That's it?"

"To tell you how much I value who you are, what you've done, what you've taught me."

Perla bites her lip. Looks toward the window.

"Perla?"

"Yes?" Perla's expression is expectant when she turns toward Tanner Blue.

"Would you tell me something else?"

"If I can."

Tanner Blue places her hand on Perla's arm. "How do you like your coffee?"

First light has come and gone at Tourmaline Beach. A second light wakes Tanner Blue. Slowly, she opens her eyes, turns around, and smiles at Nile, reclined beside her, fully alert. Gently, he places his hand on her shoulder.

"Good morning." Tanner Blue kisses him.

"You were so tired when Perla dropped you off. Now, tell me all about your trips."

Tanner Blue folds her pillow in half and rests her head on it. Pulls up the covers. "I don't know what I expected. I tried my best not to expect anything. I just wanted to tell the four people I've known the longest about something that seemed important for them to know, but I'm the one who learned the lesson."

"And that is?"

"Refuge maps its own direction."

"It might be even deeper than that, Tannerblue. Maybe everyone doesn't want or need a refuge."

"What do you need, Nile?"

"I've been giving that some serious thought. I got a high grade on my test. I needed that because I worked hard for it. My graduate advisor and I are at an impasse. He won't approve my thesis. I needed to know that. I did that sweat lodge with the Hupa brother I told you about. Never felt so clean and clear in my whole life. Then I visited the trees and collected all kinds of seeds. The breast pocket of my jacket is full of them."

"Are you going to plant those seeds somewhere?"

"I'll know when I find the right place."

Tanner Blue sits up. "Nile, would you show me your trees?"

"Why?"

"Because they mean a lot to you." She kisses him again.

"You want to see them, now?"

She nods. "How fast can you get dressed?"

He steps into his pants, shirt, and shoes. Tanner Blue throws on clean jeans and a sweater. At the front door, Nile takes her hand. "I found the book—the one Freeson sent me. It was under my bed and I swear I didn't put it there."

"What about his photo and the metal bird?"

"Gone."

"Did you find a picture of the flag you were looking for?"

He shakes his head. "One page is missing though."

The entrance to the redwood park intersects a numbered street. Walking along the pebbled road, there is a sense of adding each pace to one infinite footprint of everyone who has ever walked anywhere.

Soon, Nile stops before a wooden sculpture of a deer set back from the road. It is curled up at the foot of a redwood. Nile looks up and back. He reaches for Tanner Blue's hand as she stretches toward the sky.

"Listen." She closes her eyes. "Redwoods creak at the slightest change in wind. Maybe it's their way of talking."

"Saying what, Tannerblue?"

She opens her eyes. "They want to know why we're here."

"Let me show you my favorite tree." He steps over to one redwood directly behind the deer. Takes a small knife from his pocket and aims its point toward the tree's trunk.

"Please, don't." Tanner Blue touches the abalone-shell handle of the knife. She folds the blade into it and wraps Nile's fingers around it.

"I was going to carve our initials."

"We know we're here. That's enough."

He pockets the knife. "This is my sacred place. You're the only one who knows."

Tanner Blue wraps her arms around his waist and peers into his eyes. "Your Blackton?"

He looks up the road. "Can we walk?"

"Sure. I've always loved this place."

"I mean can we walk *there*?"

"Where? You mean...?" Tanner Blue looks toward the path.

"Yes, Tannerblue." He takes her earring from his pocket. "You might need this." After several attempts, he threads its wire through the small opening in her left lobe.

She asks, "Got your seeds?"

He places his hand on his chest and says, "Right here."

Tanner Blue looks around, seeing only Nile, redwoods, and the wooden deer. She extends her hand into thick fog, expecting to feel its weight. Instead, it is light, moist, and warm. She smiles and listens for a gentle fluttering of wings. A raven lands at her feet, blued by all the fog. Head turned toward its tail, the bird winds around in a circle, over and over again until the wind is just right for lifting off.

Endnotes

Page 89: [1]*Hidden in Plain View—A Secret Story of Quilts and the Underground Railroad* by Jacqueline L. Tobin and Raymond G. Dobard, Ph.D. (Doubleday, New York, 1999) is the source of this data. That book is based on data imparted to the authors by Ms. Ozella McDaniel Williams.
Page 135: [2] Ibid.
Page 152: [3] Sankofa is a concept originated by the Akan of West Africa, symbolized by a bird looking backward and flying forward. It represents reaching into the past in order to reclaim values that have been forgotten and need to be preserved.

Acknowledgments

I believe there is a Spirit that guides everyone and everything, and so, this work. I am grateful for the love and enthusiasm of my family, and longtime friends—Sharon, Lori, Hattie, Theresa, Wendy, Pat and Abel, and Peggy. To these I add my favorite teachers, who did indeed make a difference: Mr. Baratta, Mr. Steinfink, and Ms. Gelormini from high school, and Leslie K. Price from college. Thanks to everyone who has expressed kindness in discovering my endeavors to be a published author. I welcome into this circle every member of the audience for my writing.

Special appreciation goes to the VONA (Voices of Our Nations) and AWA (Amherst Writers & Artists) communities of writers for always holding a sacred place for me within the group.

Julia Browne, thank you telling us about Henry Ossawa Tanner and his color while we were Walking the Spirit in Paris.

Darryl Vance, thank you for lending your artistic touch to the completion of this project.

Bonniebrooke Bullock, thanks for your important contributions.

Jerry Thompson, thanks for being such a positive presence in the writing community.

Thank you for your generosity in reading the proofing copy of this book—Fred, Adrienne S. Rosa, Maureen B. Jones, and Peggy Bush. Kenny, Fred, Leah Thomas, Jackie Luckett, and Jessmaya Morales, thanks for your valuable, early assessments of the manuscript.

Kenny, thank you for lifting me up continuously, since the day that I was born.

Frederick Douglass Perry, thank you for listening deeply and ceaselessly with your poetic heart and soul—thank you for your constant half of WE—becoming—WE.

www.ingramcontent.com/pod-product-compliance
Lightning Source LLC
Chambersburg PA
CBHW02083626062 6
47169CB00003B/1017